A DANGEROUS AGE

This Large Print Book carries the
Seal of Approval of N.A.V.H.

A DANGEROUS AGE

ELLEN GILCHRIST

THORNDIKE PRESS

A part of Gale, Cengage Learning

GALE
CENGAGE Learning

Detroit • New York • San Francisco • New Haven, Conn • Waterville, Maine • London

GALE
CENGAGE Learning·

LIBRARY OF CONGRESS CATALOGING-IN-PUBLICATION DATA

Gilchrist, Ellen, 1935–
    A dangerous age / by Ellen Gilchrist.
        p. cm. — (Thorndike Press large print basic)
    ISBN-13: 978-1-4104-1006-1 (alk. paper)
    ISBN-10: 1-4104-1006-4 (alk. paper)
        1. Iraq War, 2003—Fiction. 2. Domestic fiction. 3. Large type
books. I. Title.
    PS3557.I34258D36 2008b
    813'.54—dc22   2008026292

Published in 2008 by arrangement with Algonquin Books of Chapel
Hill, a division of Workman Publishing, Co., Inc.

Printed in the United States of America
1 2 3 4 5 6 7 12 11 10 09 08

FOR CARLA

CONTENTS

1

Onward, or How Nature Took Back the Reins as Touching the Hand Clan of North Carolina during the Dangerous Years of 2001 to 2005

Miss Winifred Hand Abadie to marry Charles Christian Kane on December 21, 2001, in the Chapel of Saint James Episcopal Church in Raleigh, North Carolina, at seven in the evening, reception to follow at the Duke Inn in Durham.

That was the printed announcement, but it might have gone on to say: Formal dress. The bridesmaids will be wearing red velvet. The thirty-year-old bride will be wearing an off-white satin and lace gown that was worn by her mother and two of her aunts. The maid of honor will be Louise Hand Healy (that's me), the bride's first cousin. The bridesmaids will be Tallulah Hand, Nell Walker Bush, Sarah Hand, and Dr. Susan Clark, all of Memphis, Tennessee, and Olivia de Havilland Hand of Tulsa, Oklahoma.

The bridegroom will be attended by his three brothers and his father. Mr. Kane is employed by the Greenlaw Investment Strategy of Raleigh.

Our cousin Olivia figured it out and decided we would be the oldest bunch of bridesmaids ever assembled in an Episcopal church for a formal wedding. The red velvet bridesmaids' costumes were actually good-looking cocktail dresses with jackets we could wear later, and were being custom-made for us by a shop in Durham that specialized in that sort of thing. Winifred had lost ten pounds to fit into the wedding dress, and we had people flying in from all over the world.

Except the wedding never took place because Charles Kane perished on September 11, 2001, along with three thousand other perfectly lovely, helpless human beings.

He had been in the first tower of the World Trade Center, on the fifteenth floor, with two other young brokers, trying to set up a deal to build a new tennis club in Raleigh. The night before he had told Winifred on the phone that he thought they had it licked and he would be home a day early, in time for their mutual birthday, on the thirteenth. "We'll be able to buy a house right away if this goes through," he said. "Start looking for one and make sure it has a yard. I want some children, Winnie. I want a real life."

"We're going to have one," she answered. "Why are we having this damned complicated wedding, Charles? How did we get into all this?"

"We didn't. Our mothers did."

Their mothers had. Winifred's mother, my aunt Helen, and Charles's mother, Sally, had been friends since high school. They had given birth to Winifred and Charles on the same day in the same hospital. They were having a wedding and that was that, and Winifred and Charles were going along with it and all of us were flying in and getting giddy at the thought of red velvet bridesmaids dresses and a Christmas wedding in North Carolina with the stock market at an all-time high and all of us as rich and successful as we could be and the world before us like a land of dreams.

It is extremely hard to have a funeral when

you don't have anything to bury. It was four months after the disaster before the Kanes gave up waiting for the New York Fire Department to send them a bone. They just went on and had a memorial service on the tenth of January, and everyone who had been planning on coming to the wedding came to that instead. Winifred wore a dark brown Armani coat and knee-high boots, and I sat on one side of her and one of Charles's brothers sat on the other side, and we read poems out loud and talked about how sad we were, and the next day Charles's identical twin younger cousins joined the United States Marines.

Our cousin Olivia was the last reader. She read a poem by Yeats and a beautiful long passage from *The Tempest* by William Shakespeare. A few of our cousins thought the Shakespeare was overly melodramatic and depressing, but most of us liked it. Here's what she read:

Our revels now are ended. These our
    actors
(As I foretold you) were all spirits, and
Are melted into air, into thin air,
And like the baseless fabric of this vision,

The cloud-capp'd tow'rs, the gorgeous
    palaces,
The solemn temples, the great globe itself,
Yea, all which it inherit, shall dissolve,
And like this insubstantial pageant faded
Leave not a rack behind. We are such stuff
As dreams are made on; and our little life
Is rounded with a sleep. . . .

"You are not a widow," I told Winifred
later that night. We were sitting in the library
of her mother's house with Olivia asleep on
the sofa and an empty bottle of white wine
making an indelible stain on Aunt Helen's
cherry coffee table.

"Then what am I?" she answered. "We
learned I was pregnant last spring, and the
baby would have come a week before the
wedding. We thought it was hilarious. We
were so excited. We didn't tell a soul besides
my doctor, who had confirmed the tests. I
lost the baby a few weeks later. We were
really sad. Charles wanted to be a father so
much. We wanted five babies. We wanted as
many babies as we could get. So what am I
now, Louise? I spent years dating dopey
men who either left me or bored me or
thought I was fat. And then I turned around
and there was Charles, back in town and
working for his daddy, and it was like I'd

13

been blind all my life and suddenly could see. Now this. This isn't just some other thing that happened. It's the end of hope for me. I don't know. Maybe I'll go to medical school. I talked to Susan about it. I took the prerequisite courses when I was at Duke. I have to do something for other people now because it's finished for me. It's over." She was sitting on the sofa where Olivia was sleeping. Olivia had been made editor of the newspaper in Tulsa, Oklahoma, shortly after 9/11. She had not been to North Carolina since the attacks and had only been able to get to the memorial service an hour before it began. "The publisher actually suggested I might want to do an editorial about coming to this funeral," she told me earlier that evening. "The effects of terror on the individual, et cetera, as opposed, I asked him, to the effects on what else?"

"You aren't going to write about it, are you?" I asked.

"I hope to God I won't."

Olivia woke up and put her hand on Winifred's head and began to pat her. "It's okay," she said. "It's going to be okay. It isn't the end for you. It's a tragedy but you'll live through it. Our ancestors lost their loved ones all the time and they pulled through. We just have to relearn how to do it." She patted Winifred a few more times, then lay back down on the sofa. "Don't let me miss my plane tomorrow," she said. "I have to be back. Don't let me miss it."

She fell asleep with her hand still on Winifred's arm. It was a strong, wide hand, thick, wide fingers, her Cherokee blood. Winifred and I watched her sleep. She was so much like our aunt Anna we couldn't stop talking to each other about it. Driven, driven, driven, even in her sleep. Not that my mother or our uncles Daniel and Niall were any less driven, but it showed somehow in Olivia more than it did in them. She shone with it. She was our shining, driven cousin.

"Did you apply to medical schools?" I asked Winifred. "Did you take the MCAT? How far did you get with that? I remember Mother telling me about it, but I was gone from home and didn't pay attention to the details."

"It was six years ago. I applied to twelve medical schools and I didn't get into any of them. My MCAT scores were low and my undergraduate grades from Duke weren't all that good. I took the MCAT before I took physics. It was a stupid thing to do.

Well, I'll never be a physician. That's a dream. And I am a widow. Don't say I'm not."

"You can try again. Take the Kaplan course. I know people who applied three times before they got into medical school. It's a tough racket to break into."

"How could I do that?" She was sitting up, looking at me.

"Your daddy has plenty of money. He'd support you. Quit your job and start this month. Call the Kaplan people. You have to make a move, Winnie. If you don't, you'll get sick. This sort of thing makes people sick."

Our cousin Tallulah was pretending to sleep in a nearby room. Every twenty or thirty minutes she would get out of bed and wander into the library to join us. "People aren't supposed to die when they're young," she would say. Or "My heart is broken for you." Or "I don't know what we're supposed to do now. Maybe I'll join the air force. I know how to fly. I've been to the Middle East. I went to a tournament in Dubai. I know people over there."

"What do you want?" Tallulah would ask. "Tell me what I can do to help you." Then she would fall back asleep on the floor, with her head propped up on Winifred's knees.

16

After a while she would go back to wherever she had been pretending to sleep.

"She's hyper because she exercises all the time," I told Winifred. "If she quits playing tennis for three days, her system doesn't know what to do."

"She's a phenomenon," Winifred added. "Did you ever get to see her play in college? She won all these awards for best sportsmanship, plus being All-American three years in a row."

"I saw her once. I was awed, that's for sure, but also because she looks like Grandmother. In the face she looks just like her when she's playing tennis."

"I don't know what I'm going to do," Winifred said. "Not tomorrow or for all the days after that. I can't think of anywhere to begin."

Tallulah was waking up again. "Go to medical school like Louise said to," she put in. "The world needs people to use their skills. I'd go if I could do that sort of science. Louise is right. You have to go to work or you'll die. It's the only thing that will save you." Then she curled back up on the floor. She was still wearing the clothes she had worn to the memorial. She hadn't even taken off her panty hose.

■ ■ ■ ■

Of course my brilliant cousin Winifred didn't go right out and sign up for the Kaplan course and go back to pursuing her dreams of medical school, because that is not how shock and grief work in the world. The winter of 2002 wore on into spring and summer and the stock market didn't really recover and neither did my cousin. She went to France and stayed a while, and then she went to Italy and to Spain, and then she came back home and called me a lot in the late afternoons, but she wasn't making much progress in stopping behaving like a widow. Her parents kept giving her money and acting like she was a child, something my aunt Helen is notoriously good at doing. Meanwhile, the rest of us moved on with our lives. Our doctor cousin, Susan, joined a clinic in Memphis and changed her specialty to internal medicine and then to surgery. Olivia ran her newspaper, Tallulah Hand became the tennis coach at Vanderbilt, and my uncertain career in the arts moved on by fits and starts.

My name is Louise Hand Healy, but I work under the name of Louise Hand because my mother's sister was a famous writer and I thought the name might be a leg up in the television business. It turns out, of course, that the only legs that help a woman in television are the ones that are spread for a sixty-year-old producer with a pocket full of Viagra and breath mints.

Well, that's unnecessarily cynical. There are lots of nice men and women in the business, and I know many of them.

I've made a start up the ladder. I made three documentaries for PBS, two of which actually got on the air, one about the grave of a Roman soldier who a professor at the University of Arkansas in Fayetteville believes is the biological father of Jesus, and one about a Civil War battleground in Tennessee that had been forgotten. Only twenty men died in the battle, but sixteen of them are buried there. It looks like I'm about to become the thirty-six-year-old woman specialist in graveyards if I don't make a move soon. Maybe I should go back to calling myself Louise Healy and see if I can get a fresh start.

The events of that terrible September day are now nearly three years behind us, and I've been having epiphanies. Or awakenings, or hell, maybe I'm actually growing up at last. I think it started with a trip I made two years ago to Italy, when I was caught in a terrorist attack at Heathrow Airport. Or maybe it was the LASIK surgery I had last year that made me see like an eagle and freed me from my bifocal contact lenses. It might be the tooth-whitening procedure I had last month, or maybe it was dyeing my hair chestnut brown, mostly from despair when my third documentary got dumped on the cutting-room floor at WYBS and I decided my career had begun to tank. I don't get depressed, but that film's failure definitely cut a wedge in my self-esteem. I had to talk to a psychoanalyst to start believing it was the fault of their bad taste and not my bad moviemaking.

It was my favorite piece of work and took a year's research. I was paid twenty-five thousand dollars, minus the 10 percent that went to my agent and the forty thousand it took me to live on and travel while I did the research. I hate to tell you what it was about or you'll join the crowd who think I'm turning into a ghoul. Okay. It was about how the fall trees turn yellow and gold above the Civil War graveyards in six different towns and how the graves look when they are covered with gold and red and purple and brown and black and yellow leaves. It was really a beautiful piece of work, with cinematography by a hot young Asian who used to be the art director at Random House but quit. It had a voice-over written by my cousin Olivia. The voice-over was the names and dates and ages and everything we could find out about the dead soldiers. I'll admit Olivia and I stuck in some things we can't prove, but my God, this is art, for God's sake, not copyediting.

I couldn't believe Olivia agreed to do it for me. I flew to Tulsa on a fall day and she met me at the airport and drove me to Fayetteville, Arkansas, to photograph a cemetery there that is about as beautiful as anything can be, rows of small white markers going out from a central monument, and covered in late October by golden maple leaves. Above the graves the ancient maple trees stand sentinel, still holding some of the gold leaves, and beside an iron fence a local school bus sits and waits for the afternoon. We read the ages of the young men who died on one long morning and afternoon and night, forty miles away in a pasture by a river. Nineteen, seventeen, sixteen, nineteen, twenty-five, fifty-four, nineteen, eighteen, and on and on.

"They were hauled here in wagons after the battle," Olivia said. "There are a few Cherokees. I've been here many times. There are three more Civil War cemeteries in the area, but none as beautiful as this."

"Does nothing ever change?" I asked.

"The human race is just getting started, Louise. The cerebral cortex is only a hundred thousand years old. It's still a baby, sucking teat and eating Cheerios. We might get better, maybe even wise, if we can last another thousand years."

"A thousand? I don't know, Olivia. There's an awful lot of plutonium and uranium two thirty-five around, not to mention plagues and plastique explosives, not to mention global warming. I'm not sure we have a thousand years in us."

"There are bright minds everywhere exploring and thinking and warning," she said, looking out across the rows of golden-covered victims of the past. "Compassion and wisdom are already with us. But we have to spread the word of good things. When I wish on the first star at night, I wish for wise first-grade and kindergarten teachers. I pray for them when I pray."

"Not me. I'm still half reptilian brain, Cousin. I wish to kill dope peddlers. I'm not very advanced. I want to personally catch and kill dope peddlers and child abusers. I swear I do. I think that way, but I know it's because I watch too much television."

"You need to get laid," she answered.

"Well, so do I, for what that's worth."

"Have you seen Bobby Tree?"

"Not in a while. I still dream of fucking him. How's that for a reminder of what's really going on? He's doing well, Louise. He's out of the marines and he has a construction company. But don't talk about him. Keep cataloging the ages of these men. I want to use it in the piece."

Olivia never talks about her men. She's had some great ones, including one of the best football players in the South and a bank president. But the main one has always been the one she married and divorced, a Cherokee with black hair who was her junior high boyfriend before my aunt Anna and uncle Daniel found her and brought her to Charlotte, North Carolina, to try to turn her into a southern debutante. That's a long story and turned out okay in the end.

Bobby Tree is the name of the man she can't forget. He pops in and out of her life, no matter how much distance she puts between herself and those days. He joined the marines the last time she dumped him, and then came back in one piece and covered with medals. I don't believe that's over yet, no matter how much she won't let anyone say his name to her. If it was over, she'd be able to talk about it, or that's my theory. I don't believe you ever stop loving anyone you ever really loved. You have them there like money in the bank just because you loved them and held them in your arms or dreamed you did. You can forget a lot of things in life, but not that honey to end all honeys.

Back to my last failed video project. It lost a lot of money, including some of mine and some of my momma's. I'm sorry about losing Momma's money. That was retrograde. So now I have to find a better idea and a new backer and make a film that will get me some respect, or I have to admit I'm a second-rate journalist who'd better start learning to live in the present. And maybe I'll meditate.

Unless I get married and have babies, an idea that's starting to seem more and more like a really good one. Except who wants to bring a baby into a world that looks like it's exploding, not to mention the stock market tanking. Olivia says you really don't have to watch the news. Just turn on a financial channel and see what the markets are doing.

More about me. My father is a stockbroker. My mother is a journalist who has written three bad novels that at least got published and stayed in print a few years.

Do you remember I told you about Charles Kane's identical twin cousins who joined the marines the day after the tragedy? Well, yesterday afternoon I got a call from Winifred that deepened all that sadness. "Brian Kane just had his chin blown away in Afghanistan," she said. "Carl, his twin, is still stationed in California, but they sent Brian on because he was the star of their basic training. He was a star in telecommunications, and all he was doing was riding in a tank and running the computers to tell them where to look for weapons. That's all I know except the tank ran over a mine and blew up, and what I want to know is why we can't make tanks that can withstand mines if we are going to ride all the good-looking, strong young men around in them. They're flying him to Walter Reed as soon as they get him stabilized. I'm going there to help. So can you help me get a job in Washington? Who do you know there?"

"No," I answered. "Oh, goddamn wars to hell. Are they those good-looking blond boys with the huge smiles who were at the funeral?"

"They sent Brian over the day he finished basic training. He was a genius with computers. He was at Massachusetts Institute of Technology when he and Carl joined the marines."

"How old are they?"

"I don't know. So how about the job? Can you get me one?"

"There aren't any jobs for someone like you, Winifred. You're overqualified for anything I can think up for you to do. You'd be in a perfect place in Washington to study for the MCAT. It's nuts to give up on your dreams."

"I might do it," she said. "I might just do that. I could take the Kaplan and pick up a refresher course in organic chemistry at any of the schools near there. I'm going to stay in Washington and help with Brian as long as they need me. It's my memorial to Charles. Their family isn't very large. They don't have a lot of people like we do."

"Get a big apartment and I might come live with you, if you get a comfortable place without any cats and dogs. I'm sick of every childless woman I know having a house full of rotten spoiled pets."

"Will you try to find a place for me? I need you to help me find somewhere to live."

"I live in Baltimore, Winnie. I don't know anything about D.C. except that everything is done by pull. You need to get your daddy to call some senators or representatives or lobbyists. I heard that's how it gets done around there."

"Well, look anyway. I mean, see what you can do."

"I'll try. When will you get here?"

"In a few days. I'll call as soon as I get an airline ticket."

So of course I got no sleep that night for worrying about where Winifred would live and where she should apply to schools and how she could find a part-time job. Finally, about three in the morning, I got out of bed and made a list of contacts; then I found the Sunday papers and put them in a pile to look for apartments. I wanted to move into D.C. myself but I'd been too busy to look for anything. I'd been living for three years in a garage apartment behind the home of the style section editor of the *Washington Post*. It's comfortable but far away from any work I do. When I can find work, it's in D.C., or I have to talk to people there: small pieces for magazines or papers, or pickup jobs at television stations. Anyway, I wasn't looking forward to spending the rest of the winter driving into D.C. in bad weather and awful traffic.

"Epiphany," I told Cousin Olivia when I got her on the phone the next morning. I always call her first thing in the morning because she goes to the newspaper at dawn, so she's available. Plus, she's maybe the smartest person in the family now that Aunt Anna's dead.

"I'm going to find a place where both of us can live," I went on. "If Winifred needs to be in D.C. while she heals her wounds, I might as well help her. What else do I have to do with my empty heart and empty womb?"

"You don't have an empty womb. You have a busy life. If you want a child, go find some sperm and get to work. A baby is going to slow you down, but who knows, it might spur you on instead."

"I have to get a script ready for Allison Cardy by the tenth of February."

"Then get it done. You procrastinate, Louise. It's your Achilles' heel."

"Not always. I can stop it if I like."

"Then do it. Look, I have to go. Call me tonight, okay?" She hung up and I made a pot of coffee and went into my workroom and finished the script. By two in the afternoon I had it in the FedEx box and was on my way to D.C. to look for an apartment near Walter Reed. It was time for a change. I called Winifred and told her what I was doing and she said go ahead and don't worry about what it cost and just find something and rent it, she'd be there by the end of the week.

That was Wednesday.

"Without change, something sleeps inside us and seldom awakens." That's my mantra, when I remember to use it. I learned it from *Dune,* a book I will never stop loving. A great newspaperman wrote the *Dune* books after a lifetime of watching the world and its madness. It's the best metaphor for modern life ever written. It's our *Don Quixote* although no one ever admits it in literary circles.

I remembered it now as I set out to take Winifred into my heart and help make her well. She will be a great doctor someday, and I'll be able to feel I helped make it happen. What I forgot was that it was my empty nest that was really calling the shots. Not one I emptied, but one I never built or filled.

So within a month, while I was waiting at our empty apartment for Beds Incorporated to deliver the two new beds with mattresses and springs that Uncle Spencer and Aunt Helen were giving us for a housewarming present, who should drive up and park his Jeep and come walking up the front path to our duplex door but Carl Kane, first cousin to the dead bridegroom and brother to Brian Kane, who was being patched up by a team of plastic surgeons at Walter Reed with Winifred standing by while she studied flash cards from the Kaplan course for the MCAT. Of course, every doctor she met was falling in love with her and offering to help her get into medical school. She had never gained back the weight she lost in order to wear the wedding dress, and at fighting weight she is a major contender in the upscale looks department. I mean, she is lovely, the kind of woman a man thinks would make him look good in the world.

Carl stood at the end of the path, and I was standing in the doorway waiting for the delivery truck. I won't forget that moment ever. He had on his marine uniform, but it wasn't in very spiffed-up condition. The jacket was unbuttoned, the tie was sticking out of a pocket, and the khaki shirt was unbuttoned to the chest bone. Fair-haired men don't show much chest hair, but I could imagine it farther down. He'd been sweating, and he looked more like the antiestablishment guitar player he had been than the marine he was now.

"I'm Carl Kane," he said. "They sent me over to see if I could help. Winifred said to

30

see what you needed."

"I could use some coffee," I said. "And a newspaper. I've gotten addicted to news. So how are you all doing? Are they stitching on him today?"

"They stitched yesterday. I think he'll look okay. I've never seen such attention. Rumsfeld visited the hospital yesterday. We met him. It's busy over there."

"And you're on leave?"

"For another month. Then I'm going over. I keep telling myself not to want revenge, but what the hell, you can't help what you feel, can you?"

He stood there looking like someone I wouldn't want mad at me. Red-gold hair about half an inch long. Really nice hands. Six feet tall, intense, smart.

"How old is Brian?" I asked. "And you?"

"Twenty-four; well, we will be twenty-four soon."

Twenty-four from thirty-six is twelve. I must not think this way, I was thinking. Do not think that way, I thought.

The van arrived with the beds, and Carl went inside with me. We watched as they assembled the contemporary iron bedsteads and then unwrapped the mattresses and springs and placed them on the stands. After they left I got out the vacuum and

Carl helped me vacuum the floors of the two bedrooms, and then I opened a box and took out mattress covers and new pale blue sheets and we made up the beds and found the pillows in a closet and put pillowcases on them, and then we sat on one of the beds and didn't talk much. I hate myself at times like this. Men think they get led around by their desires. Try a biological clock.

"Let's go find me some coffee," I said. "And some eggs and toast if it's not too late, or else some lunch." I stood up.

He moved near to me and took my arm. "I'm all yours," he said. "They sent me to you."

Like who sent him? The clan, the family, the Fates? Who decided I needed a boyfriend more than I needed a job? Who remembered we hadn't had a single baby in ten years in the whole Hand clan? And it wasn't because we weren't cut out to be fruitful.

Had I taken a birth control pill in the past five days? Who knew? I'd been so busy saving Winifred, happy to be of use and not to have to think about myself morning, night, and noon. I hadn't even flossed my teeth since we made the down payment on the duplex and started ordering furniture and letting our parents pay for it, much less remembered to swallow a birth control pill when there certainly didn't seem to be much reason to swallow one.

"Is it true identical twins feel each other's pain?" I asked Carl when we were settled in a booth in a neighborhood restaurant I'd found a few days before.

"I feel this pain," Carl said. "It kills me to see the mess it made. The surgeons have been photographing me; that's weird enough. We're mirror images of each other, it turns out. Something like that. They may take some skin off my butt if they need it. He's knocked out most of the time. They aren't letting him be in pain. They've got the best doctors in the world at Walter Reed."

"They should have. I'm glad they do."

"So you make movies? Winifred said you'd made some films."

"I've made a few documentaries. I'd like to go to Afghanistan and film some of what's going on there. I don't know what it takes to get to do that. I'm small potatoes in the film world, Carl. I'm just scrabbling for a living. It's crazy. No one makes a living doing this. I don't know why I think I can."

"I bet you will. I bet you're good."

"I might be. It takes so much to prove yourself. You have to get people to put their faith in you and give you money."

"You aren't going to eat those biscuits?" He had finished his eggs and toast and bacon and was eyeing what was left of my eggs and biscuits.

"I am not. They are all yours." He took a biscuit and filled it with butter and added jelly and began to eat it. I had not taken my eyes off his shoulders and hands since we sat down and I just went on looking at them. The sexual stuff between us was so thick you could almost see it.

"What are you going to do now?" he asked.

"Wait for the movers to bring the rest of the furniture this afternoon. Stuff from my place in Baltimore. Did Winifred say when she'd be back?"

"She said to tell you she wouldn't be home until late tonight or maybe tomorrow. She might spend the night in the hospital so Aunt Sally can get some rest and our mother can leave."

"Okay."

We drove back to the duplex and went into the kitchen, where he helped me unpack some boxes. Then he touched my arm, and

34

we had a real conversation.

"Would you go have dinner with me some night?" he asked. "I mean a date, like on a date."

"You're too young for me."

"No, I am not."

"Then maybe I'll go. I'm thirty-six years old, Carl."

"So what. I'm a man, Louise. Don't play games with me."

So I didn't play any. I put my arms around him and sighed a long, deep sigh and took the man to bed and kept him there until a delivery man started beating on the door a few hours later.

Before he left to go back to the hospital, he made plans to take me to dinner the following night. "Don't act like nothing's happened," he said. "Promise you won't start all that."

"Who are you?" I asked. "I don't know who you are."

"Yes, you do. You know plenty. I'm a musician, Louise, and I'm the dominant twin. Brian is my child and my brother. He's me and now I'm going back up there and spending the night beside his bed. And then I'm going over there where they did this to him and count coup. Can you deal with all of that?"

"Twenty-four?" I said. "I don't believe you're twenty-four. I think you are a hundred."

When I was seventeen years old and having my first bad crush on a boy, my mother told me something she probably should not have told me, but all the women in our family tell things they shouldn't tell. "You don't know how easy it is to become pregnant," she said. "You cannot imagine. I got pregnant with you the day your father and I were moving into our first apartment. The bed had just been delivered and we were making it up, but we didn't even finish making it up. We made you instead. Louise, you must not have intercourse with anyone. If you think you cannot stop from doing it, you must come to me and we'll get you some birth control pills first. You get pregnant in one second, one *second*. I know you don't believe that. No one does."

I loved her telling me that. She had been drinking wine and she looked like a heroine in a movie, bending near me, her eyes big and wild and her hair curling all over the place like it does when she hasn't combed it. Plus, I liked the guilt she felt for months afterward for having told me, and her fear that I would tell my father that she had told me. He would not have thought it was funny. He's a serious man and so different from her it's a wonder they're still married. I guess they just like to do it.

And then it was true. I was knocked up. And I wasn't sorry and neither was Carl. Brian was jealous and Winifred was embarrassed, and we took to standing around the hospital bed, the four of us, trying to decide when to tell the older people in the family. We decided to have the marriage ceremony first and then tell them about the baby.

"We'll have the wedding here, in the hospital room," Carl said. "So Brian can be best man. We'll get a marine chaplain to do the service. There's a nice man in the chapel downstairs. I talked to him right after Brian got here. I know he'd do it. Come on, Louise, let's go talk to him."

Get this. I'm knocked up by a twenty-four-year-old marine on his way to Afghanistan for God knows how long. I'm going to get married without telling my parents. A baby is growing inside me. And while we are in the chapel waiting for the marine chaplain to talk to us, my cell phone goes off and Rafael Donald from PBS calls to say there's some interest in my doing a piece about the national cemeteries in the D.C. area.

I walked outside the chapel to take the call. "No," I said. "No more cemeteries. Absolutely not. Ask them if they want to do a piece about babies born while their fathers are away at war. I'm pregnant, Rafael. How's that for a turn of fate? He's a twenty-four-year-old marine. I'm marrying him this week. Then he's going to Afghanistan."

"What?" he said. "Louise, have you gone crazy?"

"Probably," I answered. "But I'm out of the funeral and cemetery business. I really won't do that anymore. Who wants to back it?"

"The station in Boston. WGBH. They're rolling in dough, Louise. It won't be about the cemetery. It will be about its history. Well, it's your idea. Your proposal."

"My priorities have altered recently."

"I guess they have." Rafael is married to an actress. She plays a doctor on *Days of Our Lives.* He worships her and talks about her all the time, even *quotes* her opinions on films. He's a terrible romantic and wonderful to work with.

"How about I send a crew to film the shotgun wedding? You're photogenic as hell, Louise. Is this marine good looking also?"

"What do you think? He's twenty-four. He helped me move the beds into my new

38

apartment. His twin brother's in Walter Reed having his face put back together after a bomb blew up his vehicle in Afghanistan. Our new metaphors and stories, all sprung from our deepest fears. I'm ecstatically happy, Rafael. I've never felt this way. I'm giddy."

"Where will the wedding be?"

"In the hospital, by his brother's bed, with the widow of a nine-eleven victim for the maid of honor."

"I want to film it. Just one camera? Will you do it?"

"Sure. But I won't say for sure I'll let you use it."

"That's fair. I'll send Carter Wilson. He's so good, when you see the pictures you'll want us to use it."

"Ten four." I hung up and went back into the chapel and sat down by Carl and thought about getting to know him, but then I decided just to hold his hand until the chaplain came.

"We'll be able to give our parents copies of the video," I told him later that night when I was broaching the idea of making our wedding into a career move. "And Brian doesn't have to be filmed at all if he doesn't want it. Winifred said it's all right with her. Do you think it's tacky? It is tacky. I'll admit that. But our parents might appreciate it."

"Mother knows something's going on. She keeps giving me looks."

"Mine's calling every day. Your mother's talking to Aunt Helen and she's calling my mother and they're buzzing with it. Maybe we should go on and tell them and let them come."

"Whatever you want to do." Carl was watching a basketball game while we were having this conversation. I am marrying a man who watches thirty hours of sports a week and I do not care. My intellectual life is in the can for the time being and I think it's funny. Right now I think everything is funny. I'm happy. I'm the Mad Hatter of happiness. I'm even starting to like Carl's music, since it's clear he isn't ever going to want to listen to mine.

"I want to get married this coming Saturday if the cinematographer can come then."

"The chaplain said he'd do it whenever we want to."

"Call and ask him if Saturday morning is good. And I'll call Rafael."

"Look at this replay, Louise. Look at that foul. My God, they should kick that guy out of the game. He almost broke the other guy's nose."

"Would you call him now?"

"It's almost the half. Can I wait until then?"

We got things set up for Saturday morning at eleven. Thursday Brian took a turn for the worse and had to be put on an antibiotic drip, but he kept saying he still wanted us to have the wedding, so we pressed on. He could talk and he could swallow, and his chin was starting to look like a chin again, even if half of it was titanium, with some plastic pieces, soon to be covered with skin from his own derriere.

I was getting the beginnings of morning sickness, which had allayed my giddiness to some extent, but not the euphoria. The euphoria was intact.

Winifred's mother, Helen Hand Abadie, had a telephone in each hand. With her right hand she was trying to reach Winifred's cell phone with her cell phone. Her left hand held the receiver to the land phone, on which she was talking to her sister, Louise. If Winifred answered, she could put Louise on hold.

"I don't know what Little Louise is doing," Louise began. "She hasn't asked her daddy for money in months. I know she doesn't have a job. So are you and Spencer paying for all this, this duplex and everything? I don't want you supporting our child, Helen, even if you can afford it. I want her to get a job with a salary if she's never getting married. She can't just live from hand to mouth forever."

"A lot of them are doing that now," Helen answered. "I think what you should be worried about is her dating that young boy. Winifred just barely admits it, but I know that's what is going on."

"You told me that last week. I don't care about that. She couldn't take that seriously. She only dates men in the film business. I think she's pretty calculating about it, Helen. That's the worry I have. That she only goes out with men to help her career. I don't know how we came to this. Not one of the girls is married. None of them have children. We had a chance and then Winifred's fiancé died and now I guess they all think falling in love is bad luck."

"Many times it *is* bad luck."

"Oh, my. Well, at least none of ours have tattoos yet."

"That we know of. Listen, Louise, someone's calling on the other phone. It might be Winnie. I'll call you back."

Helen dropped the land phone into its

base and pushed a button on the cell phone.

"Hi, Mother, it's me, Winnie. I only have a minute. What do you need?"

"Just to know that you're all right. Are you all right? What's going on?"

"Nothing. We're just standing by while they do the surgeries. It's slow. Nerve and skin grow slowly, it turns out."

"Are you studying?"

"Of course I am."

"Well, your father and I are coming there this weekend. We have reservations at the Four Seasons for Friday and Saturday nights, so we'll take all of you out to dinner."

"Oh, God, that's not good. Not this weekend. Too much is going on."

"You said nothing was going on."

"I mean, Louise is busy and you can't come to the hospital on Saturday because they have to work on Brian all day."

"We don't have to come to his room."

"It's a bad time, Mother."

"Well, we're coming anyway. Your father has to see some people so I hope you'll find time to be with us. I don't want to bother you."

"All right. Call when you get here Friday. Call my cell phone."

"We might bring Louise. She's worried

43

about Little Louise."

"Oh, God. All right. Whatever. I have to go."

Winifred hung up and immediately started trying to reach Louise or Carl, but they weren't answering their telephones.

She gave up and went over to Brian's bed and sat beside it, watching him sleep. After a while he opened his eyes and she took his hand and leaned near. "Plot thickens," she said. "My parents and Louise's mother are on their way. They've sniffed it out. It makes me believe in mind reading, the way that bunch of women can get on the scent. Once when I was in fourth grade I started doing some heavy petting with a boy who lived down the street, and my mother knew about it within hours. I think she smelled it on my hands. So how are you?"

"It's uncomfortable. I feel like I have a piece of metal in my chin. Why don't they go on and tell everyone what they're doing?"

"Because a cinematographer from WGBH is coming. I guess they think there wouldn't be room for the family."

"You want to marry me while the preacher's here?"

"Not until I see how you're going to look."

"What time are we going to have the

ceremony Saturday?"

"At eleven in the morning, last I heard."

"You think I ought to let them take pictures of me like this?"

"Sure. If you don't like it, they can edit it out."

"How do I look?"

"You look nice, for someone who's been blown up. Brian, may I ask you something?"

"Sure. Shoot."

"Do you want Carl to go over there and revenge your injury? If he could stay here, would you want him to stay?"

"I want him to go over there and kill as many of them as he can find. I want to go back myself as soon as I can."

"I hate men. You know that, Brian. All of you are as dumb as posts. But I like the way you look. I think the camera ought to concentrate on your arms and shoulders. Your shoulders really look good in your pajamas."

"Sure we can't get married?"

"I don't think so." Winifred looked into his eyes and giggled like a girl. It was the first minute of real honest-to-goodness fun she had had in months. She didn't even start feeling guilty about being happy until late that night.

■ ■ ■ ■

By Thursday night, Louise's father had decided to come along with the others to Washington, D.C.

"Secret wedding's not going to work," Carl said to his brother. The four conspirators were back in session around the hospital bed. "I vote we go on and tell them."

"Second that," Brian said. "I'm not strong enough right now to bullshit Momma. She's driving me crazy, calling me every minute. It's affecting my recovery. No kidding. I don't lie to her. It's not worth the aftermath."

"All right, then we tell," Louise agreed.

"Thank goodness," Winifred added. "I'm the one who will be blamed if we don't. I'll have both families mad at me."

At nine o'clock on Friday night, Louise and Carl went to the Four Seasons Hotel and sat down with Louise and Jim Healy and Helen and Spencer Abadie and invited them to the wedding. They had told Carl's family the night before.

"But you have to stay out in the hall while the chaplain's doing the service," Louise said, "because it's going to be filmed for PBS."

"No," Big Louise said. "You didn't do this to me. I can't believe you'd turn your own wedding into a movie for the masses."

"PBS viewers are not the masses, Mother. They are uptight matrons like yourself. No masses will see this unless I really get lucky, and besides, we haven't made plans to air it. We are filming it in case we need it for something."

"That's supposed to make me feel better?" Big Louise was weeping now. Hanging on to her husband and weeping.

"There's the baby," Helen Abadie comforted her sister. "Think about the baby, Louise. Think about that."

On Saturday morning there was fog so thick it was unsafe to drive, but by nine o'clock it began to lift and by ten the sun had broken through and was lighting up Washington, D.C., and the hearts of its inhabitants.

At Walter Reed Army Medical Center the press corps had gotten wind of the wedding, and the hall leading to Brian Kane's room was packed with people and cameras. By 10:50 the administration of the hospital had persuaded the bride and groom to move the wedding to twelve o'clock in the chapel, and the hall was cleared and ten nurses and nurses' aides were moving Brian's bed toward the elevator. "I would have done something with my hair if I'd known this," Louise kept muttering to anyone who wanted to listen.

The parents of the bride and groom were escorted from the hall to the chapel, passes were given to three networks, the PBS cinematographer had sent for help and extra cameras, and the United States of America was on its way to yet another media event and Oprah moment. Louise couldn't help wondering if the attention might not get her lost PBS special back onto a viewing schedule.

"I, Louise Hand Healy, take thee, Carl Mallory Kane, to be my lawful wedded husband, to have and to hold from this day forward, in sickness and in health, until death do us part." Louise began to cry as she finished the speech. She was still crying small, soft tears while Carl repeated the words to her, and then Brian teared up while he pulled the ring out of his hospital robe and handed it to his brother, and only Winifred, who had the most reason to cry, kept her cool and took the bride's flowers and stepped back and counted the house, listening while the chaplain pronounced her cousin and her dead fiancé's cousin man and wife.

One door closes, another door opens, she was thinking. It was the first cynical thought she had entertained since the morning of September 11, and it came like sunlight through fog, and without guilt or remorse.

"I won't let Carl go over there," Carl's mother whispered to her husband. "One son is enough."

"Not now," her husband whispered back. "We'll talk about it later."

The baby was a boy, too small and undeveloped to have access to the long line of memory that becomes the human brain, but made already of flesh and blood and subject to floods and tides and hormonal beaches, and he was having an especially creative day, having stretched out his fingers and toes a millimeter and pushed up what would become the cerebral cortex. Nature was singing, good, with what some humans have taken to calling strings, but are really parts so infinitesimal they are completely unimaginable to the human brain. Good going! That's right, keep going, they were singing, having become tired of allowing the Hand-Manning genetic pool to make its own so-called decisions for ten years now, and its gene bearers sink into cynicism and despair despite the pool's inherent gift for fecundity and joy.

"I won't marry you," Winifred told Brian much later, after he had been taken back to his room and the doctors had run off everyone except Winifred and his parents. His father had taken his mother somewhere to try to reason with her about calling the president of the United States or one of their senators about not allowing Carl to go to a war zone.

"But when you get out of here I might fuck you," Winifred continued. "Just to be mean and just because I haven't been laid in four years. This wedding made me horny. Making myself come is okay and I'm good at it because I went to a girls' boarding school. I'm an expert; I can get it done in two minutes and get back to work. It's not that. I want to cuddle up to you. That is, if you have a face when this is over and don't look too bad."

"You won't care how I look when I start in on you." Brian was drifting off into a morphine moment. The doctors had not been using much pain medication because he had told them not to, but today they'd decided they wanted him calmed down for the night.

"What if I pretend you're Charles? Just

kidding."

"Pretend I'm the Cookie Monster if it makes you good, happy — sorry, sleep. Sleep." He was drifting off, and Winifred watched him until he was deep asleep and then moved to a chair by the window and called Tulsa, Oklahoma, to talk to her cousin Olivia.

"You won't believe what's going on up here," she began when Olivia answered the phone at her office at the *Tulsa World.*

"Will I not? I've been watching it on television all afternoon. Why didn't Louise do something with her hair? She looks like a waif out of *David Copperfield.*"

"There was fog this morning. It ruined our hair. Besides, we didn't know there would be reporters. We thought it was going to be one cinematographer from a PBS station in Boston. So, how did I look?"

"Very nice. You looked good. So did Louise, except for the hair. Did she even comb it?"

"The problem is it's too long. I can't believe she won't cut it. It's so curly you can't get a comb through it. I'm going to try to get her to cut it. She's pregnant. Did you know that?"

"It's on every television news program every hour. You haven't seen the news?"

"Aunt Louise will love that. Just when she was about to get Charlotte society to forgive her for the books she wrote about them. Now they'll get their revenge."

"I wish I could have been there. Where are you? What are you doing?"

"I'm staying with Brian at the hospital. There wasn't a reception. We're going to have it later, when Brian is out of here."

"Do I detect a maternal note?"

"Not to this man. He doesn't want a mother."

"Tell me more."

"Nothing to tell."

"You need to talk to a shrink, Winifred. You don't know what you're doing. You need to get some therapy for at least six months before you go down some paths that you don't need to tread."

"You always want people to go to shrinks. I'll just talk to you instead, if you don't mind."

"I mind right now. I have to get a paper out tomorrow and we're having floods on some of the rivers that feed into the Arkansas, and besides that, the fight over pollution from Arkansas farms is red hot. Anyway, congratulations and all that to the bride and groom."

"I told Brian about you the other day. I

showed him the picture of you on the cover of *Tulsa* magazine. He said you were hot."

"Where did you get hold of that?"

"Jessie sent it to me. She writes every other Sunday. She's been writing to me ever since Charles died. Real letters. I didn't tell you that."

"My sister is an angel. I should see her more, but I don't have time to travel for fun."

"You could invite her to come see you."

"Does she want me to? Did she say she wants me to?"

"She wants you to know the children."

"Oh, God, you're getting just like your mother, Winifred. Did you know that? You can lay a guilt trip on someone so fast it's scary. So tell me about Brian. He said I was hot? I don't think that photograph looks hot. I think it looks professional."

"When he can travel, maybe I'll bring him up there to see you. He was fascinated by the idea of Tahlequah."

"He should be. It's sui generis, that's for sure. Look here, Winifred. I really have to go. I have to get to work. Give Louise my love. Give them all my love. Ten four."

Olivia hung up the phone and shook her head. Her family in North Carolina was like some traveling circus that was always showing up in town, full of magic tricks and cotton candy and games that were hard to win. One of their ancestors had crossed the Delaware with George Washington. Another had painted portraits that were hanging in the White House. There had been several generals and a governor. When she talked to them, she always had a memory of the day she found the photographs of her father and sat down to write the first letter to her aunt Anna. She had been thirteen, not even tall yet, and she had set out with a notebook and pencil to find out who she was, besides a Cherokee Indian in Tahlequah, Oklahoma.

I found out, she thought now.

Olivia went back to work on an editorial about pollution and public health.

Winifred went back to Brian's bed and looked down at the brave man and decided to call his mother and see how she and his father were doing. And what am I doing? she asked herself. Well, you don't always have to know, you know.

2

NEUROTICALLY EXERCISING PAYS OFF IN SPRING WHILE I REMEMBER CHAUCER AS I ALWAYS DO IN THIS SEASON

Journal entry, Olivia Hand, April 4, 2004. I had set out to lose three pounds, and I had lost three pounds. I had set my will to the sticking part and I'd spent three weeks working out at the gym, which is not as nice as walking in the blossoming spring in Tulsa, Oklahoma, when the first tornadoes have cleaned the air until every leaf and daffodil and automobile shines in the sunlight, but it's better than not exercising at all, or taking a chance on the tree pollen driving me to Sudafed. I'm a member of the governor's task force on methamphetamines. I know too much about chemical decongestants to take them. "They give me chills and fever," I told my physician cousin, Susan. She had called to ask if I'd heard from our lovesick cousins in Washington, D.C., and to give me the scores from our cousin Tallulah's team's matches against the University of Alabama. "It was a rout," Susan said. "Tallulah's so mad at the players that she cancelled practice for a week and took their names off their lockers."

"That's excessive," I said. "I want to tell you about these decongestants," I went on. "They give me chills and fever when they start wearing off. What's in those things, Susan? Why are drugstores allowed to sell them? I get crazy when I get these allergies. I can't believe this keeps happening to me every time the weather gets beautiful."

"What are you doing other than using decongestants?"

"Avoidance, that's the key. Stay inside and wash out my nose with a neti pot. But the main thing is I'm working out at a gym. I've lost three pounds in two weeks."

"It sounds like you know what you're doing."

"I do. Well, thanks for the diagnosis."

"I didn't give you one —" Susan began, but I had to cut her off because the sports editor was in a crisis. We're being sued for something we wrote about a high school player who got in trouble. We're being sued for reporting the news.

Plus, the cheetah at the Tulsa Zoo is sick

and I don't have anyone free to do a story on the new animal hospital. Maybe I'll do it myself.

Meanwhile we've got Keetoowahs fighting to build a casino two miles from Tahlequah, which infuriates the Cherokees, and four men arrested for a double homicide in a drug case, and the secretary of education coming down here to close a loophole in the No Child Left Behind Act, a loophole we need so we don't have to count the children of illegal immigrants who can't speak English. What else? One hundred and sixty-four billion dollars spent *so far* in Iraq, and a tattoo bill being fought over in the Oklahoma House of Representatives, plus the tobacco-peddling laws. Thirty-nine tribes to cover. Try to write editorials in the face of that. Being a Cherokee makes me suspect. I grew up in Tahlequah and my granddaddy was chief for twenty years. But hell, I love this job and I love this country.

Tulsa, Oklahoma, in the Interior Highlands, rolling hill country given to drought and tornadoes, the last place white men *thought* they didn't want, so they gave it to the Cherokees and the Pawnees and it became the Cherokee Nation and the forty-sixth state of the union. There are now thirty-nine federally recognized tribes in the

57

state, all fighting to sell cigarettes and build gambling casinos.

I love this barren, rolling country. Folsom and Clovis hunters were here hundreds of years before the Cherokees arrived. When I was a child I hunted arrowheads with my granddaddy. I have a shelf of arrowheads and pottery shards in my grandparents' house in Tahlequah. When I go home to visit, they are right where I left them, on a shelf by my bed.

Back to my diet. I lost half the three pounds by the seventh day; then it slowed down, so I went home to Tahlequah to spend the night. Whenever I have anything hard to do, I go spend time with Little Sun and Crow and Aunt Mary Lily. It makes me strong to be in their presence.

"So what is going on in Tulsa now?" Granddaddy asked as soon as we were settled on the porch chairs with our glasses of iced tea. He had given me the most comfortable chair and taken the second-best one for himself.

"What is the news in Tulsa now?" he asked again.

"The cheetah in the zoo is sick and they're taking it to the new animal hospital. Big fights over zoning and the construction on

Yale Avenue. The Tulsa Ballet has a new director. They're calling up more of our National Guard units to go fight this war."

"We have to fight our enemies."

"The sons of the Midwest always fight our wars. The sons of the poor and the sons of the Midwest and the South. Not a single congressman or senator has a child in this fight. Well, don't get me started on that."

"Why do they not send their children?"

"Because it's dirty, dangerous work and they don't want their children subject to military discipline."

"The world has changed very much in my lifetime." Little Sun held out his hand to her. "I am proud you have this important job to tell people what is happening."

"The ones who need to know don't read the newspaper, Granddaddy. They get their news from television and the radio."

"I wish I could think of ways to help you."

"You help me by being here. You help me by being who you are so I can measure myself by you." I went to him and kissed him on his sun-browned cheeks. I ran my hands across his fine, strong shoulders and touched his thick gray hair. I was home for the night. I was okay and the world was what it had always been and I didn't need to go starving myself either.

■ ■ ■ ■

I slept that night in my old bed with the leopard-skin print sheets and pillowcases and comforter that Aunt Mary Lily had bought me when I was fourteen. My pottery shards and arrowheads were on the shelf by my bed and I took down a worn steel gray arrowhead I had found in a bend of the Illinois River about seven miles northeast of Tahlequah. I was with Granddaddy and my first cousins Tiger and Roge, and we found a lot of stuff that day, but nothing as beautiful and perfect as the stone gray arrowhead. The following Saturday, Granddaddy and Roge and Tiger and our cousin Sunny and I had taken the arrowheads we found to Professor Cramer at the Department of Anthropology at the University of Tulsa, and he said they were Folsom arrowheads, hundreds of years old and very valuable.

"If you like, you can give them to us and we'll keep them here," he told us, but I was selfish and wanted to keep mine for myself. Roge gave him two of the ones he had found and Tiger gave him one and a pottery shard, but I kept mine for myself.

"We have a museum in Tahlequah," I told

him. "If I give them to anyone, I'll just give them to it."

I went to sleep holding my arrowhead and dreamed all night about being out on the river. A big brown bear came and picked me up and carried me very carefully in his paws. I wasn't afraid. I knew he had come to help me.

When I woke the next morning, Grandmother was cooking bacon and toasting biscuits. Three mornings a week she makes biscuits from scratch. On the other days she toasts them in the toaster with so much butter you have to tone it down with blueberry jam.

I didn't completely ruin my diet at breakfast that morning, but I used up all my lagniappe calories for the next week. Scrambled eggs and toasted biscuits and two pieces of bacon and homemade blueberry jam and coffee with real cream. "I dreamed a bear came out of the woods and picked me up and carried me," I said. "But I wasn't afraid. He was holding me like I was very precious. He was quiet and just holding me and carrying me."

"Where were you in this dream?" Granddaddy asked.

"On the Illinois River at the gravel pan

where I found the steel gray arrowhead. I was on the edge of the pan and the bear came out between the trees and picked me up."

"He is telling you to protect the woods and the river," Crow said. "Anyone could interpret that dream."

"I'm doing everything I can. I can't help it if I think there are two sides to every story, even environmental issues."

"There are not always two equal sides," Granddaddy said. "Right and wrong are real, and you can see them if you believe what your heart tells you. You spend too much time with people who want everyone to like them. Because you have to sell the newspaper, you forget what you are supposed to do."

"You're right. I think about my job. It's amazing how corrupted we all become. Scared. Then corrupted. We're all running scared at the paper. We have to sell advertisements, so we have to have circulation. Even Big Jim has been running scared. He's got six children. He sold his birthright to buy that paper and now he doesn't know how he'll educate all those children or how they'll make a living. It's hard making a living now, Granddaddy. When people don't have land, they can't always make a living anymore. Or they have to do slave work no one wants to do."

"You have land," Crow said. "You do not have to be corrupted or write things you don't believe."

"Oh, God," I said. "I knew I ought to come down here. I knew I wasn't thinking clearly."

Crow came over to my side and put her hand on my shoulder and then leaned down and put her head beside mine. "You come to give me pleasure in seeing you," she said. "You come in answer to my prayers."

Later that morning I took my laptop computer off to a wooded spot near the pasture and spread a blanket on the grass and wrote the best editorial I'd written in weeks. Then I folded up the blanket and walked back to the house and kissed everyone good-bye and drove back to Tulsa to go to work.

Here is part of the editorial. This is the part I really liked writing.

The United States is in a war that ranges from Indonesia to parts of Russia. It is a conflict that will rage for many years and many generations, and we should be getting strong and wise to meet this challenge.

Instead we are getting fat and wasteful, and many of us don't take care of our children properly or set good examples for them with our lives. They are being raised by television and blogs and computer chat rooms.

We build casinos instead of schools. We drink alcohol in front of our children and let them watch us solve our problems with drugs instead of lifestyle changes.

We undermine our marriages and homes with alcohol and drugs, and we are in debt, as a nation and as individuals, to such an extent that we have industries springing up to teach us how to borrow money more efficiently. The United States borrows three billion dollars a day from China!

We are living as though there were no tomorrow.

I don't know how we are supposed to turn this around, but here at the *Tulsa World* we want to try. Starting Monday the paper will carry a section called "How to Make It Better." It will be a series of essays by physicians, nurses, teachers, psychiatrists, business leaders, lawyers, bankers, engineers, electricians, carpenters, preachers, priests, firemen, policemen, feminists, antifeminists, and any other people of use and worth that we can find to write for us. Send us your suggestions. Send us your essays. It is spring.

Let's get our heads on straight and out of the sand and our facts in line. Our ducks in a row, as my grandfather used to say.

"It needs cutting," my publisher, Big Jim Walters, said. He's a six-foot-seven-inch genius with a head of curly black hair and a booming voice and presence. He bought the *Tulsa World* with money his daddy left him. He spent all the money he had and borrowed more. "Hell, I've got twenty years to live, if that much," he said. "I don't want to die thinking I didn't get a damn thing done to save the state where I was born."

Big Jim is a man who smokes and drinks and eats three meals a day. He went to Vietnam when he was seventeen by lying about his age. He came home and went to the University of Tulsa, where he majored in history and geology and spent a year in law school. He married a girl he met in English class, a classy-looking little girl who was the first person in her family to go to college. She sat in the front row and paid attention and held up her hand for every question.

Big Jim sat behind her and fell so deeply in love that he read every page of every novel the professor gave them to read. When the semester was over, he asked the girl for a date. A month later he asked her to marry him.

They have four sons and two daughters.

I love working for Big Jim and I love arguing with him and stalking out of his office and eating dinner with his family and taking his children out for heart-to-heart talks.

"I know it needs cutting. How about the series? May I do it? We'll have to pay for some of the pieces."

"How much?"

"I don't know yet. It will have to be on a piece-by-piece basis for a while."

"No, it won't. You can have two hundred tops for each piece. Get a standard contract and stick to it, no kill fees. Pay the subscribers a hundred if they send something in. I don't want to pay anyone unless we pay everyone."

My editorial ran on Sunday. By Monday afternoon there were ninety-six e-mails offering to write essays. By Wednesday we had sixteen articles set up, beginning with one by a physician who runs a weight-loss program in Muskogee, to be followed by a piece by a retired United States senator about the importance of being an informed voter. That would be followed by an engineer writing about how to buy a house, to be followed by a local banker talking about debt. Then a piece by a television weatherman about preparing for tornadoes and what to do if one comes.

The series was a huge success and was given credit for the rise in circulation we saw in May and June.

So the year wore on and the war in Iraq got worse and more confusing. We were depending on the Associated Press for feed, then Knight Ridder and the *New York Times.*

In June, Big Jim and I flew to Kuwait and spent a week talking to generals and embedded reporters; we learned nothing we couldn't have found out from the Associated Press feed, and I went home more confused.

"It's not confusing," Big Jim kept insisting on the flight back to Tulsa. "You want a big picture, and the big picture is hundreds of years old and worldwide. You need to study maps." He kept getting out a map of the Middle East and studying the geography. "Think of it as Texas, Oklahoma, Arkansas, Missouri, Mississippi, Louisiana. We need maps of religions, sects, Shiite and Sunni strongholds. Look at Lebanon, for God's sake, sitting right on top of Israel, Syria looming to the side. We need maps of where the oil is. It isn't confusing. It's about oil. It's about oil and geography and ports. Nothing else. To believe otherwise for a moment is to *become confused.* Well, maybe it's also about nuclear power — plutonium's been found in Iran, they're mining it, and they're processing it — but that's secondary. *It's about oil!*"

"If I didn't work for you, I'd marry you," I said. "I'd take you away from Linalee. You're the only person I ever knew who could italicize words when you talk."

"Our advertising revenue was down for the year. That's three years in a row. Are you aware of that?"

"Then fire me. I've gained four pounds since I became editor. I have fat on my waist. My pants are too tight. I haven't gotten laid in twenty-six months. I wish you'd fire me."

"It's not your fault. No one reads, so they don't buy newspapers. We need better maps, Olivia. I want to put some maps of the Middle East on the front page, with oil fields and refineries and ports. I want the ports in red. I want maps on the front page *and* the editorial page whenever we write about the war."

I put my hand on top of his large, powerful, fat hand. I patted his hand until I fell asleep. In my sleep I dreamed about the geography of the Middle East, the mountains of Afghanistan, the nuclear bombs in Pakistan and India, the port of Dubai, Syria looming, Lebanon, Israel, Palestine, Iran, the oil, the oil, the oil.

The 747 in which we were crossing the Atlantic Ocean would burn enough fuel to lose 20 percent of its weight by the time we got to the United States. Gasoline had reached $1.79 a gallon in Tulsa while we were gone. In another few years it would be almost $4.00, and the cost of printing and distributing the *Tulsa World* would almost have doubled.

Live in the present, I told myself each night before I fell asleep. Nothing lasts forever. Nothing ever did. I really need to get laid, but it's so much trouble. I've had good men and I didn't keep them because I'm too selfish and I won't put out the effort. I'm going to end up living with pets if I don't realign my priorities.

So I made it through the winter and the spring and summer by doing what I hoped

69

was valuable work in the world. But I was lonely and I didn't know I was lonely as fall came to Oklahoma and the elections of 2004 drew near. There is nothing more dangerous than being lonely without knowing you are lonely. I was getting set up, that's for sure. I was about to be used.

3

DON'T LET YOUR
BABIES GROW UP TO
BE COWBOYS

Saturday, October 30, 2004. It's three days before the election, and trying to run a newspaper under these circumstances is like shoveling fleas, a metaphor Abraham Lincoln used to describe being president of the United States, which is what this election is about and/or for. Which one of the disparate groups of people who not only don't want their oxes gored — they want to graze up everybody else's fields, oxen, cattle, horses, oil, sheep, water, air, you name it — will win? This election is about keeping what is mine and getting some of yours. And so what? What else is new in the human race?

Things are looking up in the newspaper world. As of today our circulation is forty-eight thousand, up two thousand from last year, either because of my essay contest, Big Jim's maps (we now have school contests to draw them, and we publish the winners in the Sunday paper), the election, or the war. People like to read the names of the dead, I guess, or the commentaries. Who knows what they like? Anyway, circulation is up two grand, but what good does that do me this week? We are so besieged by e-mails, telephone calls, and letters to the editor, we can't even print the news.

There are other things going on in Oklahoma this week and I'm trying to put some of that news on the front page, but my staff is fighting like a pack of wild dogs for their separate and bitter agendas.

Not to mention the Cherokee faction, of which I am a fully licensed, if not full-blooded, member. I'm not full-blooded because my mother fell in love with and was impregnated by and briefly married to an aristocrat from North Carolina. She ran away from him before I was born and had me in Tahlequah, Oklahoma, where she thought I belonged, not thinking about North Carolina's being the beginning of the Trail of Tears, or about anything else, for that matter, since she was only twenty years old when my birth took her life — something nineteen years of psychotherapy has finally cured me, I guess, of thinking was my fault. My birth ended her life; that's a fact. But I didn't mean it to, nor would I have chosen to end it. No matter how much I know that intellectually, I still suffer guilt. Everyone has his burdens; that's my main one.

As for the presidential election of 2004, the Cherokee Nation is split. If national polls show George Bush and John Kerry neck and neck, the Cherokees are for once in lockstep with the nation. Here's how it's split: the young people and dope addicts and malcontents and trial lawyers and social workers and some of the veterans, against the old people and rich people and doctors and the rest of the veterans. I don't think I need to waste words telling you who is for whom. Breathe in, breathe out. What they are fighting now is one another. Everyone is so mad. If I printed the really interesting letters to the editor, I would have mayhem to answer for. Of course the Cherokees are always fighting, plus farmers versus oil people and small towns versus Tulsa and so on.

Has anyone ever written about what great lovers Cherokee men are? I wish I dared, but then I'd have to move and the Cherokee women would say, Why don't you write about what great lovers we are? and I'd say, Because I don't desire women, and then the lesbians would jump on me. Public discourse, not good now. Some days I think I ought to quit this job. I could freelance like my cousin Louise. Of course she had some family money. Well, so do I, or I did until I bought that land down on the river. That's a sinkhole for my salary, but at least I don't keep men.

Sunday, October 31, 2004. A double-witching day. At six this morning I threw on my clothes and went down to the office to start combing through the *Chicago Tribune* and the *Denver Post* and the *Seattle Post-Intelligencer* and the *Washington Post* and the *Oklahoman* and the *Arkansas Democrat-Gazette* because I wanted to see if there was anything I needed to recap in Monday's paper, and also because I couldn't wait to see what other editors were pushing for in the last days before this fucking election, which isn't going to make one goddamn bit of difference in the real foreign policy of the United States of America because when anyone becomes the commander in chief, this bunch of — because we are free — still wild (thank goodness) people will storm Washington, stop paying taxes, or do what they have done so many times before, which is actually go out and vote and elect a

Congress from the most extreme bands of the other side if they don't like what their newly elected president does. I love the dark, sweet heart of the American people, and I trust them to keep the ship of state sailing on through any storm, and I'm going to write an editorial for tomorrow's paper saying so.

So I was sitting at my desk, hungry, drinking coffee and eating unsalted sunflower seeds, when my old love Kane Malloy comes in the door and just stands there. I haven't seen him in three months, and in two seconds I'm sounding like a sixteen-year-old girl. What can I say? I love the man. I've had two loves in my life, and this is the troubled one. So he's married. Put me in the jail and throw away the key. I didn't know he was married the night I met him at a party at the Tulsa Country Club (a party for a golf tournament he won the following day). And it's not my fault that his fat, rich wife sits in their house in Oklahoma City and lets him roam. Roaming — that would be a good nickname for Kane. And I'll tell you something else: he would love me to the exclusion of every other woman on the planet if I would be his mistress, but he'd never leave Arlen Vinci Malloy because of her money and their children. The facts are the facts, but I know damn well he loves me. Everyone in Oklahoma knows it, as well as everyone in Arkansas, where he's from, and anyone anyplace where old football players play golf, and definitely everyone in heaven, where we have to justify these things.

"What are you doing in town?" I asked, and sat up straight and pulled my shoulders back and down, à la Pilates class, and pushed my lips out and pulled in my stomach, à la Tahlequah High Cheerleading Squad, 1984, not coincidentally the year I found the photographs and learned my father was the brother of the famous writer Anna Hand of Charlotte, North Carolina. It was the year I began to believe I was somebody special and could do anything I dreamed of doing.

"Selling bonds, baby, and spices for my daddy. Same thing I'm always doing."

"Don't give me that. You don't show up in Tulsa three days before the election to peddle bonds. I know who you run with, Kane. So what's your role, revving up the old professional athletes in general or just the old football heroes? You could have saved the time and money. This state is all red and it's sewn up unless the student population surprises me by actually voting, which it won't except for the born-agains."

"Oh, baby," he begins. He takes a step nearer to my desk, and I get a whiff of the pheromones and I might as well go on and take off my clothes, since he can do this to me on the telephone, let alone when he's standing in my office in his perfectly tailored gray slacks and his soft Italian long-sleeved polo shirt — as if clothes could cover that incredible body, as if anything could hide that power and those reflexes and the sheer unbelievable intelligence of his physical being, not to mention the gentleness and pain and courage and intensity, the stillness and quiet and truth, of his great, sweet heart.

"I'm going to talk to some people for the governor. We need some poll watchers. But that isn't why I'm here. I came to see about you. Are you still mad at me?"

"Sit down. I was never mad at you. I get mad at myself because of you and then I take it out on you. You're married. I will not have an affair with a married man. I am not going to spend another Christmas waiting for you to come over in the late afternoon. I've done it, Kane. I can't do it anymore."

"Well, I love you. You know that." He hung his head, not that it's possible for him to hang his head because his shoulders are so perfectly designed that they hold his head up like an emperor's or a king's. He is the most beautiful man I have ever seen in my life, and he's half-Chickasaw, from the tribes in the Mississippi Delta, so I recognize as well as love him. Half-breeds, both of us, Irish, Celtic music running with the Indian blood. Mixed blood, the best, the wildest, purest strain there is.

What the hell, I decided. I might as well go on and fuck him — carpe diem and all that. Life is short and we're all doomed one way or the other.

"You're looking good," he said. "I love it when you don't put makeup on your face."

"I got up at five to come down here. How did you know where I was?"

"You weren't at home and I know you like to work in the early morning. I couldn't sleep, knowing I was in the same town as you, so I came out looking for you."

"How's Arletta, or whatever her name is?"

"Arlen. She's okay. She's been sick."

"How's your golf game?"

"It's been better. Look here, Olivia, how about going out to eat breakfast with me? I'm starving to death."

"There's a hotel in the next block that's open now — the café, I mean. All right, let's go." I got up from my desk and put on my old tweed jacket, pushed my hair back from my face, took off my reading glasses, and came around the desk, and he put his body around me and held me as though I were a bird in a golden retriever's mouth, and I let him hold me because why not, for God's sake — I love the man.

Around noon we got out of bed and he called the Republican headquarters and I called the newspaper and we got dressed and went our separate ways, to pretend to work, and then we came back to the hotel and got sad as hell the way we always do. Here's how we worked the sadness.

"I can't leave her because she's sick."

"You can't leave her because her father is part of the southern Mafia and he'd have you killed."

"That's also true."

"So the Mafia is backing President Bush?"

"I don't know who they're backing. I'm backing him because I believe in what he's doing. I'm not arguing with you, Olivia. I have a lot of friends who don't agree with me, but I can't help believing what I believe, any more than you can help believing what you believe." He hung his head again. It always got to me when he dropped that amazing chin down from that amazing neck. He's so still and he just keeps on being there, six feet three inches of a man who was Rookie of the Year with the Chicago Bears and would have been the greatest running back they ever had if he hadn't lost his right knee to gravity and a right guard from Champaign, Illinois, who afterward became his best friend and used to caddy for him while he was learning to play golf so that he'd have a reason to live. He won the Oklahoma state championship one year after he bought his first set of clubs.

"I'm glad you hurt your knee and had to quit playing football," I said. "They might have torn up your whole body if you'd kept on playing."

"They'd have had to catch me first." He didn't take his eyes from mine. His eyes were the darkest brown I've ever seen, except for an old chief I knew in Tahlequah who also had the strange, pure power this man I'll never stop loving has or contains. *Contains* is the better word. It's this reservoir he never taps in front of me. "What have you been doing, Olivia?" he asks. "I tried to call you at least twenty times last month, but no one would put me through."

"I'm going out with a newspaperman from Fayetteville. He used to work for the *New*

York Times. I've been fucking him just to spite you."

"I don't fuck her."

"Yes, you do. You liar. You fuck Arlette and half the women in Oklahoma and maybe Mississippi and Tennessee and Alabama. No, I'm sorry; I know that isn't true. Jesus Christ, Kane. It's a couple of days until the biggest election of the last twenty years, and you have to show up and do this to me. Make me jealous of shadows. Make me sick with dreading when you leave two days or two hours from now and then I'm back to taw without a paddle and no one to eat dinner with."

"What's his name?"

"William Finney. It's nothing. He plays golf, but he's not any good."

"Do you still have my putter?"

"Yes, it's at my house. You want to go over to my house and get it? Come on, let's go. The main thing wrong with all of this is the rented hotel rooms. That always makes me so sad, but then everything about this is sad. In real life, nothing makes me sad. How dare you make me sad."

"I don't know, baby. I don't mean to. I know I don't."

So we went to my house and I got his goddamn putter out of my umbrella stand and

81

gave it to him, and then I took him back to the Republican National Committee head-quarters and I went back to the office and got to work in earnest. It was going to be a long haul until the polls closed on November 2, and I had work to do.

Sometime that afternoon I had an epiphany. It isn't just Kane and his breathtaking sweetness and his body, I realized. I am wonderful too, goddamn it, amazing and unprecedented. I took the life I was given — not that much different from the lives around me in Tahlequah, Oklahoma, although the genes were very, very good, I guess — and I made a hugely successful career. My grandfather had been a chief of the Cherokee Nation and my grandmother was uneducated but strong and wise, and they had loved me and taught me to be strong.

All those blessings given to me, and out of that, I, the love child of a Cherokee girl and a young man from the upper middle class of North Carolina, had brought my talents to fruition in those strange years in the United States, years of upheaval and change, and become the youngest person ever to be editor of the main newspaper in Tulsa, Oklahoma.

So what if I wasn't very good at relationships over the long haul and had fallen for a married man? That's not much of a stumble in a life that's been mostly success.

"Don't do this to me again," I told him that night. I looked him right in the eye and kept saying it. "I won't be nice the next time you show up in my office or call me or do anything else to get me to be a fool. You are married. You have children. Go home and act like a man, Kane. Get the hell out of here."

"I'm sorry you feel that way, baby."

"Leave."

Then he was gone and I went back to the office and back to work, waiting to find out what headlines we were going to need in what was now the next forty-eight hours.

"I'm sick of this goddamn election," my best friend, Thomas Keys, said. He is second in command at the paper and a stalwart in every way: a veteran, a war hero, a one-armed wonder in the brains and ability departments. "I don't even want to know the results of what the American people in all their diversity and craziness and half-educated guesses and real and imagined vested interests decide to do about the future of this, my beloved country. Long may it wave and so forth."

"How are you feeling, aside from that?" I asked. I was at my desk with my feet up in the second drawer, trying to get a knot in my leg to quit twitching.

"I'm doing okay for a man who hasn't had a good night's sleep in a week. I keep waking up thinking I'm supposed to do something."

"Write me an editorial for Wednesday's paper about the lessons of history."

Tuesday, November 2, 2004. Election day and goddamn it if I don't run into my ex-husband standing in line at Creek Elementary School, where I go to vote. They had some really good art on the walls where we waited in line. One especially good combination poem-painting was called *A Fast, Fat Squirrel.*

I was halfway to the door of the room where the voting was taking place when I spotted him just turning in his ballot. Bobby Tree, the first boy I ever fucked and the only man except for Kane that I ever loved. You don't forget your first love. Nothing is ever again that fast and fat.

A minute later he was beside me with his hand on my waist and all that goddamn indescribable sexual stuff that comes out of his five-foot-ten-inch Cherokee body like snowmelt in the high mountains in early May. He used to take me to the Rockies in spring to watch the snow turn into rushing rivers, then take me down the rivers in a canoe.

I was having my second epiphany in a week: in some vast illumination I realized I could love two men at once. That is how men do it, love more than one of us. I want them both, but not together the way men fantasize about their women. I want Kane then and Bobby now, and maybe that's how you keep it in balance, or maybe it's the new vitamins I got in the mail from Andrew Weil, or maybe it's just this damn election.

"Where are you going when you leave here?" Bobby asked. "Come have coffee with me. I've been missing you. Every time I read the paper, I think of you and how proud I am of everything you do."

"Okay." That's what I said. Words were never a big deal between me and Bobby Tree.

"I'll wait out here in the hall," he said.

"Look at the pictures," I said. "There's a fast, fat squirrel you'd really like."

So I vote and turn in my ballot, and ten minutes later I'm at Alfred's Coffee Nook, eating sweet rolls and crying on Bobby's shoulder about every goddamn thing in the world. An hour after that I'm screwing him, and then I was three hours late to the office on Election Day and I didn't even apologize or give a damn. The last editor of this paper was a staggering drunk and didn't show up one-tenth as much as I usually do. I'm sick of the election anyway. Who gives a rat's ass which political party is at the trough?

"There'll be a real attack now," Bobby said, and I believed it when he said it because I believed it anyway.

"As soon as this election's over, they'll attack, and this time there'll be a nuclear element. No one can protect a country as free and open as the United States. They've got so many Mexicans in Oklahoma now you can't count them, and even more in northwest Arkansas. And Muslims in all the colleges. Plus any black or white kids that are pissed off and want to do damage. I just pray it will be in a city. After that, there's an outside chance the United States will wake up and get serious about protecting itself. I hate to tell you that, but you asked me what I was thinking." He sat back on the bed, his body as beautiful and tanned as it had been when he was young, his black eyes boring into me, loving me. The most seductive thing about Bobby is he really loves me, no matter what happens; I never doubt that.

"Things are going well at work," he said. "You ought to come out sometime and see the things I'm building at the old fairgrounds."

"I will," I said, knowing I probably wouldn't do it. Nothing ever came of Bobby and me fucking each other. We'd been too many miles together and the trip had been too rocky.

So anyway, that's how I spent the first week in November, fucking both of my old boyfriends, which is really unusual because I haven't been fucking anyone much for a year. William Finney is mostly talk. Feast or famine. Don't judge me on my sexual behavior this one week. Most of the time I live like a nun and work twenty hours a day and give to charity and try not to hate my fellow man. Olivia de Havilland Hand, remember me. My story is far from over.

Things are also far from over between me and Bobby Tree, who started off loving each other in the days when we were just branching up to be real human beings.

The election happened. Nothing came of it except the usual. Life went on. I worked all Thanksgiving Day and went out Thanksgiving night to see a movie my crew had been begging me to see — a film called *Sideways,* which they all thought was hilarious because of a scene with an actor we know from Mississippi running naked down a street, trying to catch his wife's lover.

I had hardly taken my place in the ticket line when I saw Bobby a few places in front of me, wearing his old blue and black plaid flannel jacket, his black hair curling all over his head.

"Twice in one month," I told him. "I guess that settles it."

"I'll buy you a ticket," he answered. "What do you want to eat?"

We bought buttered popcorn and Diet Cokes and went inside and watched the film, and then we went to my house and spent the night.

"I used to know how to be happy," I told him. "And so did you. What's happened to us?"

"I've loved you all my life, Olivia. I'll always love you. All you got to do is let me be with you. You don't have to change yourself for me. I know who you are."

"Yeah, I do need to change. I have this new idea I got from yoga. It's about the ana-hata, the heart chakra, this imaginary place in your chest that you open up so you can let people in and love them."

"Could we go to bed now?" he answered. "I got up at dawn and couldn't find a thing to do except go look at a project we've got going on Webber Street. I didn't even call my dad and step-mom until right before I went out to the movie."

"Let's stop acting so goddamn pitiful," I said, giggling. "Let's go to bed and see if you can still make me come."

4
A FAITHFUL LIFE

So, for a lot of mysterious and not-so-mysterious reasons, Bobby Tree and I made up for good. We didn't talk about it much. We just decided to go on and try to be happy. Who knows, maybe having the world seem like it's coming apart draws people to the things they really love. Maybe it's fear. Anyway, Bobby Tree and I settled down to make a new start. We'd been loving each other since we were fifteen years old, and we knew each other's past. "Look at it this way, baby," he told me. "Sooner or later we'd get back together. Why wait till we're old and gray?" And he pulled me close to him until I could feel his body taut and fine against mine, and the same old music started playing. "Dance with me. I want to be your partner. . . ." It has been our song since the first time I heard it on the radio, riding in Bobby's old red pickup toward the river to take the canoe from Pinewood down to Five Feathers on the east fork of the Big Black. I hadn't been going out with him more than a week and already we were getting in trouble.

"I'm going to Fayetteville to a cheerleading camp," I'd told my grandparents. "I'm driving over with Bobby Tree because I don't want to go on the bus. Why — why are you looking like that?"

"Where you going to stay over there?"

"At the university, in their dormitories. I did it last year. Don't you remember?"

"You didn't go riding there in a car with a boy," my grandmother said, and my grandfather was about to get into it too when Bobby drove up in the yard and got out of the truck, came up on the porch, shook my grandfather's hand, and started talking to him about fishing.

So we got away okay, but I forgot to take my cheerleading costume, so when I got back, there was hell to pay. Except by then Bobby and I had been down the Big Black from Pinewood to Five Feathers and on down to Reserve and spent two nights in the woods in sleeping bags, and I could see how good he was at everything in the world, from making a fire without looking like he was doing a thing but breathing, to holding me against him like there wasn't even air between our hearts, and it was done. Not that we hadn't already loved each other for weeks before going off to be alone with the earth and make our bond.

Except all that was twenty years ago, and now he was making a living building houses around Tulsa and I was the first woman editor of the *Tulsa World* and our lives had moved further apart — but not really, not in the place where the life of the heart and soul is lived.

"I want to do it right this time," he said. "I want your grandfather to do a blessing for us in Tahlequah, and have the dances and the fertility rites and wear the deerskin robes. I have a headdress that was my uncle's. He gave it to me right before he died."

"Granddaddy's too old to do a blessing ceremony. We'll go to him and ask him who to get to do it."

"And we'll have children. I want a child, maybe more than one." He was so proud, sitting beside me at the kitchen table with his shoulders back and his head lifted. He was a grown man in his prime and it was time for me to be a woman, and I had already made up my mind that that was what I wanted to be. I wanted it because I wanted him, and without children, without sons and daughters, there was no real love, no real partner or dance, only new ways to be lonely and alone.

"Then let's hurry up and get that going," I said. "Because I'm already almost too old to have babies, and I don't want my children having old people for their parents."

"Is that so?" he said. He was finishing off his eggs and bacon and moving in without doing anything but changing his eyes, and I got up from the table and started trying not to give in to it, but hell, I love to fuck the man.

"I'm sorry I'm late," I told the reporters who had been waiting in my office for fifteen minutes when I got there at ten thirty. "The goddamn traffic on Harvard Avenue was so bad I started to get out and walk."

"You want us to go back to the courthouse and do another piece on the Hardin trial?"

"Yes. You didn't need to wait on me. Go on over and see if the jury's coming in, and interview anyone you can grab. This afternoon I need someone to cover the soccer games at two junior high schools. Take a photographer. Jim and Beth are on the rag about circulation again. Jim read something

93

about the growth in population in the county and he thinks we need to make the local news more prominent, and I think he's right. So what? Are you mad at me for being late? I just moved in with my ex-husband, all right? I'm sorry. I'm human."

"After all," Charles Ott said, and he came around to my desk and gave me a kiss and handed me his expense report for staying in the hotel with the jury for three days. "It's okay, Olivia. We're cutting you slack. Just don't let it settle into a habit."

"It might," I answered. "What the hell. I'm in love and we're going to have a blessing ceremony as soon as we can get it going. You're both invited. It takes two days. You ever been to one?"

"No," they both answered. "But I guess we're going to now."

"You're going to cover it. One of you is. I'm going to make it page one and the cover of the living section on Sunday. Jim wants local news, I'm giving him local news."

Only it wasn't going to be that easy because nothing ever is, and if it were, we wouldn't want to do it anymore because the real enemy of human beings is boredom. Or so I told myself when I started throwing up on Saturday morning, just when I'd arranged to take the weekend off so Bobby and I could go down to Tahlequah and see Grand-daddy and get things going for the blessing ceremony.

"I think that's what happens when you get pregnant," Bobby said. He was sitting on the edge of the bed, patting my back. I didn't feel all that bad, just groggy and sleepy and more or less wanting to be left alone.

"Go get one of those pregnancy test kits from the drugstore," I said. "Buy two kinds and come back as quick as you can. And some Seven-Up. Get me some Seven-Up or a Coke."

I fell asleep and drifted into a wonderful strange sort of dream about being on the pier at Lake Wedington. Bobby was in the water saving a bunch of babies that had fallen in. He would get one and hand it to me and I'd put it in the basket, and then he'd get another one and hand that one to me. The babies weren't in danger in the water. They were floating, just waiting for him to swim over and pluck them out and hand them to me. It all happened in slow motion, and the sun was shining and it was warm and we just kept on working, getting out the babies, until he came and sat back on the bed and woke me.

"I wish we could do the test now, if you don't mind. Do you feel like getting up?"

"Read the directions."

"I already did. You have to urinate — I mean, pee."

"I know what *urinate* means." I turned over and started laughing.

Then I sat up on the edge of the bed and tried to get the blood to go back to my brain. I went into the bathroom and urinated into the container and stuck in the swab and walked back into the bedroom, and we watched it turn dark blue.

I felt nauseated for another hour, but Bobby fed me soda crackers and Seven-Up, and by eleven thirty I was dressed and we were in the Nissan driving to Tahlequah to make my grandparents ecstatically happy. I already knew how they would act. Aunt Mary Lily and Grandmother would be worried and happy. Granddaddy would be mystical and happy. He was a mystical man who had been chief of the Cherokee Nation for many years when he was younger. He was Little Sun of Wagoners, son of Morning Sun and Flowering Morning. My grandmother's lineage was even more interesting, but she didn't like to talk about it as she was part Arapaho.

"I've seen pregnant brides at blessing

ceremonies," Bobby said. "I think you'll look good, Olivia."

"I hope we get it going before I'm as big as a house. The office will buzz for weeks with this. Well, at least Jim can't fire me now, no matter how much I goof off. I could sue him for millions if he fired me because I got pregnant."

"He won't fire you anyway. The paper's twice as good since you took over." He reached over and touched my hand, and I hated the Nissan Maxima and wished we had the pickup so I could cuddle up beside him and feel him driving and see his dick getting hard and his breathing slow when he started wanting me. That's our history, and now our history is going to be something new.

Granddaddy was waiting in the yard down by the gate, pretending to be inspecting the fence, but he'd probably been out there for an hour. We picked him up and he rode in the backseat to the house. "What took you so long?" he asked. "Your grandmother's been watching the clock since breakfast."

"I was throwing up. I'm pregnant, Granddaddy. Bobby and I are going to have a baby."

"Now you're railroading," he said. "It's been a long time since we had a baby around here."

Then Mary Lily and Grandmother came out to meet us and we told them our news and they started going crazy.

We went into the house, and the day went by like an hour while everyone gave us advice. In between we talked about the blessing ceremony and how many people we could ask to come and manage to feed, and how we'd have to find places to sleep for the ones from far away. Even when we were leaving, Grandmother and Aunt Mary Lily were still hovering over me, throwing in bits of childbearing advice. Mary Lily was worse than Grandmother, and she had never had a child. She had, however, had a long friendship with the main midwife in our tribe. She had helped at hundreds of births as she reminded me about a hundred times.

"Mary Lily's been doing exercise classes at the meeting center," Grandmother said. "She is very full of life lately."

"We are proud of her," Granddaddy added. "She is going three times a week. See how slim she is becoming."

"Kayo's nephew has been coming around," Grandmother said.

"It's tai chi," Mary Lily said. "It's for the heart and soul. We have this Vietnamese girl who comes here and shows us how. In China they do it every day. Even very old people go outside on the green spaces and do these exercises. It isn't anything to do with Kayo Manley's nephew, Philip White-horse. Don't tell her that, Momma."

"Okay," Grandmother said. "It isn't, then."

I hugged Grandmother and then I hugged Mary Lily and asked her if there was anything I should be doing that she hadn't already told me about.

"You need to go see Miss Roisan and get some herbs to take away the sickness," Mary Lily said for the tenth time. "She makes sachets you keep by the pillow and they take away the morning sickness."

"She needs to eat soda crackers and let the baby settle into the womb," my grand-mother added. "She doesn't need any sachets. I had plenty of babies without sachets. It only lasts a few weeks."

"I have to get back to Tulsa, is what I have to do," I said. "Aunt Lily, you get me some of those sachets and mail them to me. Will you do that for me?"

"Yes, I will get them tonight." She moved near to me and I thought, as I often did, of how fortunate I had been to have these people love me.

Bobby and Granddaddy walked to the car together. They had decided to use our pasture for the blessing ceremony so people in Tahlequah wouldn't have to travel far to come to it.

"We haven't had a frost," Bobby said. "Will the chiggers be gone?"

"It will be all right," Granddaddy answered. "We'll spray the pasture, and people can stay in the hotels on the highway instead of sleeping on the ground. It's no use to sleep on the ground in this new time."

"I want to sleep on the ground," I said. "Or else we might just as well have the ceremony in the basketball gym."

"Some can sleep on the ground and some in tents and some in the motels on the highway," Granddaddy decreed. "We will do this soon even though it's winter."

"There isn't a hurry," I said. "We've already been married, Granddaddy. It's not like this baby is illegitimate. Everyone knows we were married before."

"Then get married again tomorrow," he said. "Do this right away."

"We will," Bobby said. "We'll do it this week."

On Monday we went to the courthouse and got a license, and on Wednesday afternoon we got married in my house with half my reporters and editors there, all laughing and being cynical, and Bobby's father and his new wife and some of our old friends from Tahlequah. We were married by a circuit judge and then we all went to dinner in a Mexican restaurant and then dancing at a cowboy bar and then Bobby and I went home, and the next day he moved all his things into my garage and storage shed and it was done. I was Mrs. Bobby Tree again and our baby was growing in my womb, and in six weeks we were going to be blessed by my grandfather, Chief Little Sun of the Cherokee Nation, in a ceremony of such meaning and power that nothing would ever part us again.

We had decided to put off the blessing until after the Christmas holidays. Bobby's fledgling construction company was in the middle of a building restoration, it was money time at the paper because of Christmas advertisements, and Granddaddy wanted time to call in his chits with some dancers and medicine men from around the state.

There are strange energies and currents in the stream of human events, and many things no one understands and only seers and artists notice or record. Little Sun had watched such currents all his life, had been drawn to notice them and keep them in his awareness so he would be prepared to help when help was needed. It had made him a great chieftain of his people and a great father and grandfather to his children. It also made him a hard man to live with for his wife, Crow, whose intuition and wisdom were at least equal to her husband's, or maybe even keener.

Little Sun had just told her he was going into town to talk to a Chickasaw medicine woman who had moved there a few years before from Mississippi.

"I want Spotted Horse Woman to stay in the big tent with me for the first night."

"No. You are asking her other things. Tell me what you have dreamed."

"No, I don't wish to talk about it here."

"Then I will go with you today to talk with her."

"Walk outside with me to feed the mare. Put on the coat Mary Lily gave you."

Crow walked to him and past him out the door. She had put a knitted medicine shawl over her shoulders and had pulled her long hair back into a braid. She went down the stairs and stood in the yard waiting for him.

"I have dreamed for six nights that we are

being pursued by wolves," Little Sun began. "Olivia is small and you are carrying her, and Mary Lily is in a tree, waiting for us to get to her."

"Where are the other children?"

"They are not in the dreams. I want to call to our sons, but I must keep moving. It is hard to move across the difficult terrain; there are deep gullies and the ground is hard packed, as though there had been a drought for many months."

"I believe your dreams," she said. "I have had feelings also, many days in the mornings. I want to call Olivia and talk to her and see if she is too busy. She is always too busy. It is not good to be busy when the new baby is finding itself in the womb. What should we do? Does Spotted Horse Woman say what to do?"

"She says we should send our thoughts to surround her." He paused to see if Crow was looking at him yet, but her gaze was still toward the ground. "Spotted Horse Woman is making prayer wheels. Nothing will keep this from coming. We must wait and see. Worrying about it does not change its course. We must keep moving and be strong for when we are needed."

"I want to tell Olivia about your dreams."

"No."

"So she will be ready."

"She knows. If we know, she knows also."

"She is too busy. She might mistake it for something else. At Flaming Rainbow they said seeing is nothing unless you see clearly. How can she see clearly at the newspaper office with all that news of evil things coming in from all over the world at every moment?"

"We could drive over there tomorrow and take her some fresh eggs and cream."

"Yes."

Then I will not be able to ride with Kayo, Little Sun was thinking. All my life I have had to give up riding to drive in the automobile and dodge the other machines on the highway.

"Then we will go. Will you be satisfied now?"

"I will." She turned her face and looked up at his and he saw in her eyes the lovely young girl she had been when he first met her. It was their secret and no one could take it from them, and they did not need to speak of it because it was written in their hearts forever.

That afternoon, Bobby Tree got the letter saying his reserve unit had been called up for active duty. The letter had been mailed a week before from the Pentagon in Washington, D.C., and had been forwarded from his old address.

Bobby had served four years in the marines when he was in his twenties, after he and Olivia had split up. He had spent most of that time in a unit in North Carolina and had met some of Olivia's cousins and visited in Charlotte with Olivia's father, Daniel Hand. When his four years were over, he had signed up for the reserve unit to get the $356 a month he was paid for going one weekend each month to a base in Nebraska to keep his skills up-to-date. He was a marine mechanic, training that proved invaluable in the construction company he started when he got out.

He had begun with building driveways and doing landscaping and drainage projects. This required heavy equipment and he was able to buy secondhand tractors and repair them and keep them going.

In the two years before he and Olivia found each other again, he had moved on to restoring houses in the old, historic parts of Tulsa. He could do wiring and plumbing and even oversee roofing. He had a sixth sense for any kind of machinery or tools, and men liked to work for him because the tools they needed were always good and in working order.

By the time he and Olivia were married, he had a business that employed seven people full-time. He had made one of his cousins into his partner, a gesture of good-will that was going to pay off in the coming months when he would be gone.

Bobby was in the hallway reading the letter when Olivia came in from the newspaper. It was six thirty and dark outside. The cold weather Little Sun had been wanting had come in the night and enveloped eastern Oklahoma, gripping it like a gray fist. Cold and damp and deep, Olivia thought as she turned the key. And three months of it to go. Well, maybe two and a half, although you can't trust March not to be worse than February.

She stepped into the hall and saw Bobby with the letter and knew not only that it was bad but also what it said. She hadn't been reading newspapers all week for nothing. If they were calling more reserve units, they would call the ones from the Midwest. The South and Midwest always fought the wars, farm boys and high school athletes, poor boys and sons whose folks worked for a living, the sons and daughters of the beautiful small towns of America. That's who went to war and that's who shed the blood.

Bobby handed her the letter. "Don't worry," he said. "If I have to go, all I'm going to do is keep the goddamn trucks running. Over there the fucking things will be full of sand. I can't believe . . . well, to hell with it. I'm an American. I took the money and now I have to do the work."

The letter said he had to report for duty on January 30. The blessing ceremony would go on as planned on Friday and Saturday, January 14 and 15.

Little Sun and Crow and Mary Lily and their neighbor, Kayo, were planning the ceremony without consulting Olivia and Bobby. "They are very busy," Little Sun kept saying. "We will do this so they do not have to worry."

Olivia was taking an antinausea pill every morning and was working like a demon at the newspaper, trying to show how unaffected she was by the changes in her life. Bobby was finishing a project and getting things ready for several more. He would take a computer with him and would weigh in on the construction work, at least as long as he stayed in the United States. He did not expect to be in the United States for long. He had a skill that was needed in Iraq, and he knew where he was headed as soon as he read the letter.

Is this the price of love? Olivia asked herself a hundred times a day. Why should my happiness and joy be taken from me for a war I cannot justify, although perhaps I do understand why it must be fought. All of that is nothing but words until your flesh and blood is in the game. Now I'm in the game and I cannot think clearly or believe anything I hear or anything I read. It's down to Bobby getting on an airplane and flying into a war zone, where he might be killed at any moment, no matter how much he tries to tell me he will be in safe places getting sand out of the steering apparatus of machines. Let machines fight the wars. That's all I know for sure that I believe. I should be one of those nuts who write the Pentagon all the time and tell them how to run the war.

"Dear Secretary of Defense: Please hurry up and finish designing the machines that will fight our wars and keep our beautiful young men or women from getting in the way of bombs or bullets.

"Dear Secretary of Defense: Please let my husband out of this obligation. We didn't know there would be a war when he signed up to be in the reserves. Yours sincerely, His wife. Postscript: I'm pregnant. Doesn't that count for anything? What are we fighting for, by the way? If it's oil, why not say it's oil and quit all the rhetoric?"

Christmas passed and Olivia and Bobby gave each other presents and pretended to be cheerful. They spent Christmas Eve with her family in Tahlequah, and Bobby went hunting with her uncles and cousins on Christmas Day. Then they drove back to Tulsa so Olivia could get to the newspaper office to check the layout of the after-Christmas sales advertisements.

Olivia was being very careful in her editorials about the war. "I have to write one saying my husband is going over," she said. "But I decided to wait until you get orders. Just saying you were called up with your unit isn't powerful enough."

"What will you write?" Bobby asked.

"I don't know. I'm not privy to what the government knows. I keep thinking the entire Senate voted to go to war. What do they know that we don't know? What were they told?"

"We know they are politicians."

"No, it's more than that. What do you think they know?"

"That we have to make a stand. That's what war is always about, Olivia. Making a stand, drawing a line."

"Where does it stop?"

"It won't. It will always be that way. You choose to be a warrior or you choose to be a slave."

"You really believe that?"

"Yes. I do."

"I know you do. What if you die?"

"I won't die. I'll be fixing tractors and tanks."

"I don't believe it."

"Try to believe it."

Because they were busy at the newspaper, Olivia was not leaving Tulsa for the blessing ceremony until Friday afternoon. The entertainment editor, who had been assigned to write the story about the ceremony, had volunteered to drive her so that Bobby could go in the morning and help set things up for the sweat tent. Bobby had become very quiet as the days leading up to the blessing drew near, very tender and careful when he made love to her, more like the very young man she had loved than the grown man she had remarried. They hadn't been talking much these past few weeks. Bobby wasn't talking to anyone, and Olivia was doing her lashing out on the typewriter, although she wasn't publishing what she was writing. She was just getting it down on paper. Underneath and beyond all that, she was strangely happy and content, sure Bobby wasn't going to die, sure in some deep, strange way she didn't understand or care to examine. I'm the denial queen, she told herself. Well, it works. It's worked so far.

In New Orleans, Olivia's half sister, Jessie, had just heard from their cousin Louise what was going on with Olivia and Bobby and was at her computer frantically e-mailing their father, Daniel, who was on a hunting trip in Africa. "What is the veld?" Jessie had asked Louise on the telephone that morning. "He said they were going to the veld."

"It's a Dutch word for wilderness, but he'll get the e-mails if you keep sending them. If you don't hear back, call me and I'll pull some strings up here. He'd go crazy if he knew this was going on and he wasn't here to help."

"Why didn't Olivia call me?"

"I don't know. All I know is that they're having a blessing ceremony, some special thing the Cherokees do occasionally for people who get married."

"Well, I'll find Dad. She's pregnant; that's the main thing. I love Bobby Tree. The only time I ever knew her to be really happy was when she was with him."

"She's pretty happy being editor of the Tulsa newspaper. I can tell you that."

"You can't come home at night to a newspaper office."

"Well, actually you can."

"Good-bye, Louise. I'll call you back tonight."

Jessie walked through her beautiful house to the room she called her office and sat down at the computer and heaved a sigh and began to try to figure out how to get hold of her father.

Outside the windows of the elegant spare room, with its oak floors and Oriental rugs and handmade shutters painted pale blue to match the walls, a nest of mockingbirds were making a racket in a grove of cherry trees. It was cold weather for birds to be so loud, but these mockingbirds were acting as if it was spring.

Jessie got up from the computer and went to the window, where she stood watching the birds fly madly from the feeders on the ground to the bare branches of the trees. I love families, she thought. I'll write a poem about those birds and give it to Olivia for a wedding present. And I'll give her some of Grandmother's silver. Grandmother should have left part of it to her anyway. I miss Olivia. What good does it do to have a sister if I never, never see her? Well, at least I'll let her know I'm standing by. What would I do if King went to Iraq? I would die of fear. Maybe not. Maybe I could be strong. Olivia will be strong. She's the strongest woman I have ever known.

Jessie went back to the computer and sent several more e-mails to her father, and then some to both of his business partners, asking them to help find him pronto. Then she wrote an e-mail to her cousin Tallulah in Nashville. "Dear Tallulah, Olivia's husband, Bobby Tree, has been called up to go to war. Also, Olivia is pregnant. Try to come to the blessing ceremony they are having. You can stay in the motel with me. We need to close around her now. Say you'll come. Love, Jessie."

An hour later she turned on her computer and there was an answer from Tallulah. "I'll try to be there. I knew about the baby but not about Bobby being called up. Damn and double damn. My team finally won two matches in a row. They are driving me crazy. There isn't a single girl who really wants to win. I'll finish this year, but then I'm quitting. I'll join the air force or go to law or medical school. I won't coach these losers. I need Olivia to prop me up, not the other way around. Love, and thanks for the update, Tallulah."

Little Sun and Crow had invited three hundred people to the blessing, not counting Olivia's and Bobby's friends in Tulsa and some friends of Bobby's in the reserve outfit. The yard and pasture had been sprayed for chiggers, although the cold weather had probably killed them already. Extra beds had been put into the house, and twenty rooms had been rented in a motel on the highway. Two cafés in Tahlequah were making food and bringing tables. A medicine man from Tunica, Mississippi, was coming two days ahead to set up the sweat tent and oversee the fire sites. He had ordered cedar chips for the fires from Indiana in case he didn't like the cedar trees in Oklahoma. His name was Deer Cloud, and Little Sun had known him for thirty years, since he was a very young man and had come one winter to teach at the Cherokee school in town.

There would be the sweat tent for the groom and his close friends and his father.

114

The next morning the blessing would begin at dawn and last all day as the visitors each came to the bride and groom and offered their blessings and prayers and handmade amulets against evil. A group of Mary Lily's friends were at work on a quilt for Olivia. Crow was making the deerskin dress that Olivia would wear. It was being bleached in the old way, and three women were beading the sleeves and collar with beads that had been on the dress Crow had worn in her blessing with Little Sun.

Everything was very quiet and orderly as the Wagoner family prepared to bless the union of their daughter with Bobby Tree, this time for good and this time for the making of children instead of for selfish reasons.

Little Sun and his friend Kayo had gone to the spring at the back of the pasture to clean away debris and get it ready for the morning of the blessing. It flowed into a cold, clear pond that stayed full of water even during severe drought. Bobcats, mountain lions, deer, and many other creatures had come there for water in the first years that Little Sun owned the land. Now the surrounding woods had been thinned and not so many creatures could be found there in the early mornings. Watercress and mosses and mint and small blue wildflowers grew on the banks in the spring. Hickory, oak, and locust trees were all around it, their roots feeding on its underground streams.

"It is too cold for Olivia to bathe here because she is pregnant," Little Sun said. "She can walk in up to her ankles and bathe her face and hands. Then Bobby can walk in beside her and do the same. I have talked to Deer Cloud and he agrees this is enough. If it snows, it will be beautiful. I will not worry if it snows."

"Snow would be good," Kayo agreed. "Snow would be a blessing if it comes."

They sat down on two large granite rocks that Little Sun had flattened many years before, and Kayo got out a pipe and lit tobacco and they smoked in peace, without talking. Then they got up from the rocks and shook the crooks out of their legs and began to walk back toward the house. It was still ten days until the ceremony, and already they had done almost everything that needed doing. Now it was time to sit quietly and think about all they would say to bless the union.

When they were almost to the barn, Little Sun stopped on a rise of land and turned back toward the pond. "Deer Cloud said it would be good to make a mound for Olivia and Bobby to sit on while the blessings come. He said it would be all right to make it with a tractor, since there was not time to make it by hand. What do you think of that idea?"

"The banks are above the pond already. It would not take long to raise part of them."

"Deer Cloud said his father built one in the shape of a serpent when he was married. It is still there, on the land where he was raised. He says the rain does not harm it because his father planted grass seed that had been brought to Mississippi from North Carolina two hundred years before. He will send me this seed if I decide to build it."

"We could not get grass to grow that fast. We would have to use sod. My nephew has a landscape company. He would bring us the best sod he sells."

"You think we should do this?"

"I think we should begin this afternoon. Can you see this in your mind? Show it to me."

Little Sun raised his hand and pointed to where the line of trees came to a point in his vision. "There, along the bank, before it begins to curve."

"I see it. I will call my nephew and tell him to send two men to help us."

"Grandfather is building us a ceremonial mound," Olivia told Bobby that night. "It means he is worried about you. I am glad he's worried. He has powerful medicine. It has kept me safe always, and it will keep you safe when you are gone."

"I want his medicine," Bobby answered. "I would not mind dying in a battle. But to be blown apart by a bomb — that is not a death a man can imagine. And I would not like to leave you alone with our child. It weakens me to know how much I don't want that to happen."

Crow and Mary Lily were helping with the construction of the mound. Spotted Horse Woman and her two sons were there, as well as Kayo's nephew and two of his workers. Little Sun's tractor had been equipped with a shovel, and there was a smaller tractor Kayo's nephew, Philip Whitehorse, had hauled over on a flatbed truck.

"It is the rattlesnake, Uktena," Spotted Horse Woman was telling Mary Lily. "Very powerful for fertility and purification and for power. The earth island they build today will stand for many years. It will be a testimony to the power of the earth to protect those who love and serve the world."

"It's too long," Crow said. "They should not have tried to make such a long one in such a short time."

"More men will come in the afternoon," Mary Lily said. "I think many people will be here soon to help."

Little Sun and Kayo and the men continued with their work until afternoon. At four o'clock they stopped to eat the food Crow had brought to the spring.

As they sat on blankets eating corn bread and fried chicken and fried winter tomatoes, they looked back toward the barn and saw a third tractor carrying three men headed their way. Behind the tractor was a Jeep with four more men. The men included two of Little Sun and Crow's sons and five of their friends.

"Sorry we couldn't get here sooner." Little Sun's eldest son, Roper, climbed down off the tractor. His younger brother Creek got out of the Jeep and joined them.

"Why didn't you call and tell us to help you?" Creek asked.

"Because we didn't need your help at first; only now we need it because Kayo and I have made the earth island too long. I am very glad you have come."

"Then let's get started," Roper put in. "There are two more hours of light. Let's work while we can."

"We can use the car lights when it's dark," Creek added. "We don't have to stop when it gets dark."

"We need to build up the tail to match the body," Little Sun said. "Come and look at the plans Kayo made."

Kayo had drawn his plans on paper, then built a scale model on the ground: a long snake of dirt with its tail curled where the bank curved around the spring. The younger men took over now, and Little Sun and his old friend Kayo watched as they began to measure and plan.

They worked until after twelve o'clock that night, and then all the men went home and came back in the morning. By the evening of the second day it was done: a thirty-foot-long serpent with a diamond on its head and black eyes made of stones Spotted Horse Woman said came from the mountains of North Carolina, stones that were very old and sacred. The diamond on the head of the snake was made of a piece of quartz.

"I am a sergeant in the United States Marine Corps," Bobby was saying to Olivia.

"I have been called to duty by the commander in chief and I will go and do my work. There are five companies in my battalion. I might be in the infantry or I might be in the Headquarters and Service Company. I didn't ask and they didn't tell me. Even if I'm in an H and S, I could still be sent out as support for an infantry convoy. There's no point in telling you I won't be where there's fighting."

"When you come back, will you quit the reserves?" she asked.

"I can't say what I'll do when I get back. I'm a marine, Olivia. I take it seriously."

"So do I, Bobby. So do I." She moved her hand to his chest and kept it there. She vowed to stop talking about it to him. "Let's have supper," she said. "Let me cook supper for you."

Little Sun and Kayo were sitting on the porch steps, looking toward the pasture to admire the almost completed earth island. The serpent's eyes glowed in the early morning light and the diamond on its head stood out in perfect proportion to the body.

"We have the sidewinder," Little Sun said. "But we still must find a trickster. Who can we get to play the trickster?"

"No one wants to be it anymore. When I

121

was young, we all wanted to put on the red and orange leggings and the bells, but no more. I have asked all the men who are working on the earth island."

"We could ask the women."

"I do not like it played by women. We might have to ask someone from Tulsa. I know dancers there from the powwow."

"No. I want a local person. I will ask my lawyer, Mr. Horan. He likes to be in plays and he sings at his church. He might do this for me."

"He isn't Cherokee. How could he do it?"

"He would do it well. I have seen him in one of his plays."

"The trickster is difficult to do."

"Will you do it?"

"No. It is too much in my soul. I fear it too much to impersonate it."

"Then we will go this afternoon and ask him to do it."

That afternoon the two men put on white shirts and bolo ties and went into town to talk to Little Sun's lawyer, a forty-five-year-old Harvard Law School graduate who had settled in Tahlequah to handle oil and mineral rights for the tribe. Tim Horan had handled Little Sun's money and investments for fifteen years. Only he knew the

122

extent of Little Sun's holdings and he never told. Little Sun lived in terror that his children would find out they were rich, and then would quit their jobs and start drinking, a fate that had befallen many of the young people of the Cherokee Nation.

The lawyer stood up when Little Sun and Kayo came into the room. He offered them coffee, and the secretary brought in a tray. Then Little Sun told him what they were asking him to do.

"I know about the trickster," Tim said. "I have a painting of him by Charles King. Let me see." He went to a wall of books and took down a book of Native American history. "Here it is." He began to read: " 'Not only does the trickster defy the flesh-and-blood boundaries of animal identity, he also refuses to fit into the mental categories we use to understand the world. Stupid and wise, reviled and respected, dangerous and clownish, the trickster reveals that the world is a confusing and mutually contradictory place. He is what we all hold in common — life itself.' "

"See," Kayo said, "this is how it is. Olivia's husband has been called to go with the marines to fight this war. Just when they have settled into their life. This is the trickster's work."

"I could play it," Tim said. "I could make a costume like the one in my painting. Wait a minute. I have a photograph somewhere of my painting. I want you to look at it and see if this is a good costume."

He found the photograph and the men bent over it, admiring the beadwork and feathers and crazy split headdress, half-black and half-red. Then the three of them went downtown and ate lunch and talked about oil drilling and whether the tribe should build another casino on the river.

"Granddaddy has talked his lawyer into being the trickster," Olivia told Bobby that night. "Now our blessing ceremony is turning into a festival. He and his buddy Kayo are going crazy over this. I think everyone in Tahlequah is in on it now."

"They love you there. They're proud of you."

"They're proud of *you*. You were the athlete and the rodeo star."

"I was thinking about the trickster the other day. I feel like this war is the trickster. I don't mind going. It's just the sand I dread. I dreamed the other night of trying to get sand out of a goddamn truck engine. It was embedded in the grease and oil. Every time I would get a piece of the engine cleaned off enough to work, I'd look and another part would be wrapped in coils of grease penetrated with sand. We had lectures and drills about it all weekend a few months ago. Well, hell, that's why they call it work. I got a letter yesterday about the pay. It's better than I thought it would be. It's based on the years of service and years in the reserve and rank. I'm a master sergeant now. I'll actually be making some money and there'll be things for you and a bonus for leaving. I don't know what that will be yet."

The telephone was ringing. It was the newspaper. They needed Olivia to rewrite the morning's editorial because of some new developments in Iraq. She went into the room they used for an office and worked until twelve thirty, then fell into bed beside Bobby and willed herself to sleep. The trickster is here now, she told herself. I should write an editorial about the trickster. I'll write it after Bobby leaves so he won't have to know how sad I am and how scared.

The Friday of the blessing ceremony, Bobby got up at dawn and kissed Olivia good-bye and drove to Tahlequah to begin his part in the rituals.

Olivia and her entertainment editor left at eleven that morning, a truck carrying the photographer and his assistant following them. What had started as a cover story for the living section had now become a feature of the Sunday magazine. The story had everything: Native Americans fighting America's wars; a young woman editor left alone while her husband goes off to war; an ancient blessing ceremony in Tahlequah with the Cherokee Nation in attendance.

The sweat tent was set up at the far end of the pasture to the north and east of the sidewinder mound, as people were beginning to call it, although Mary Lily kept correcting them and calling it the earth island.

The medicine man from Tunica, Mississippi, had the fire going by the time the sun rose on Friday morning and was feeding it cedar dust from time to time. Bobby and his friends would not enter the tent until almost dark that night, and the man from Tunica wanted the ground underneath the fire to be hard and packed when that began.

After he had the fire going in the sweat tent, he began to build the fire for the dancing. Little Sun had cleared a place in front of the earth island and had brought firewood and stacked it neatly in sections. His sons had gathered kindling and pinecones and sections of cedar and cedar branches.

Olivia's father had called from an airport

126

on the East Coast to say he would be there by dark and not to meet his airplane because he might have to charter one from Memphis.

"Even though I didn't call him, I knew he would come," Olivia said when she arrived at the house and Crow told her the news. "He has never let me down and he never will. I want him to be here for this. Well, let me see the deerskin gown. I have dreamed of it." Crow and Mary Lily and the wives of her uncles led her to a room on the back of the house where the beautiful white deerskin dress was spread out on the bed. It was beaded and embroidered with flowers and birds and animals, with stars and the sun and the moon and intricate designs and mandalas and good luck signs, and it had pleats in the side.

"Crow did it every night until it was finished," one of the wives said. "She did nearly all the work herself."

"Thank you, Grandmother," Olivia said. "I thank you with all my heart for this wonderful gift."

"You will wear it all day tomorrow," Crow said. "But you can put it on now and wear it also."

Olivia took off her shoes and shirt and long pants and nylon hose, her jewelry and brassiere, and stood before the dress. She picked it up and let it slide down over her body. Then she turned and faced the women.

"Oh," they all said. "Oh, yes," they murmured.

At three in the afternoon the dances began. Olivia had changed back into her regular clothes and put on boots and tied dancing ornaments around her ankles. With the women following her, she walked out to the pasture and saw the earth island and could not keep from crying when she saw it.

Bobby was with the men, sitting in a circle before the island. The hired dancers were putting on headdresses and bells, and the musicians and drummers were preparing to perform. Olivia and the women sat in the places readied for them. The drumming began and the first dancer leaped into the circle around the fire and began to dance; one by one the others joined him. It was a dance of fire and then a dance of war. It was a dance of warriors, and it was for Bobby Tree.

The pasture slowly filled with people. By the time the war dances were over and the dances for the blessing of the bride and groom began, there were three hundred people spread around the pasture watching, standing mostly, but some were sitting on blankets and some on folding chairs.

The dancing went on for hours. At the house were tables laden with chicken and venison and bowls of fresh and cooked vegetables. There was corn bread and biscuits and thick flatbread made of beans, and many desserts, as most of the visitors had brought some sort of pie or cake or muffins. There were bowls of fruit and pastries made from the hard green apples that grow in that part of Oklahoma. There were pitchers of iced tea and plenty of hot coffee. The cold held off until around six at night, but after the sun went down people began to come to the house and stay longer and longer, except for the ones who were dancing.

Around eight o'clock the medicine man called Bobby and his three best friends and Little Sun and several of his sons and nephews to come to the sweat tent and begin the purification rites. Little Sun was not going to stay long in the tent because of his age, but he wanted to be there for the beginning of the ritual.

At ten o'clock everyone in the pasture began to come pay their respects to Crow and Olivia, after which they left, promising to come back the next day.

The last visitor was preparing to leave when Olivia's father, Daniel Hand, came in the front door and went to her and embraced her and stood beside her, holding her hand. "Am I too late for the sweat tent?" he asked. "I wanted to be here for that."

"Come with me," Little Sun said. "I will take you. They made me leave because I am an old man. Now, with you here, perhaps they will let me come back in." He took Daniel away from Olivia and led him from the house.

They would not return until morning.

At eleven o'clock, Olivia went to her old room and got into her bed and fell asleep and slept until dawn, which was not early, since it was deep into winter in Oklahoma and the sun didn't show until almost seven in the morning.

When Olivia wandered into the kitchen, her father and grandfather and Bobby Tree were already at the table, eating ravenously after their night in the sweat tent.

"When will you put on your dress?" Bobby asked.

"As soon as someone gives me some food and gets ready to be dazzled," she answered. "Well, I'm glad you all made it. I'm glad no

130

one is dead."

The men looked from one to the other, but they would not answer. The sweat tent was sacred and the ritual was not shared with women.

At nine that morning, Olivia dressed in her ceremonial dress and put on the cowrie shell bracelets and anklets that had been in the Wagoner family for a hundred years. Then she walked beside her groom out to the freezing pasture and sat on deerskin hides before the earth island, and the medicine man blessed them, and Little Sun did his blessing in Cherokee and then in English, and then people began to arrive and came one at a time to talk to them and give them presents and wish them a happy life.

By noon the ceremony was over, and everyone was back at the house warming up and eating the leftover food from the night before.

"It should have started at dawn, but it's too cold this time of year," Olivia kept telling people.

"It's going to be in the paper next Sunday," she told other people. "Be sure and get the paper and look for it."

"Thank you," Bobby kept telling people. "We thank you for coming and supporting us." He kept adding, "I'll be all right. I'm a mechanic. I might have to go on patrols, but I'm not an infantryman. I won't be in the line of fire unless they attack the motors of the machines."

"Sand repellent," he told others. "If you think of any way to keep sand out of eyes and engines, let me know."

"No, they don't have chiggers," he told one little boy. "But I'm sure they have something worse. I'll let you know when I get back."

Bobby and Olivia had meant to drive back to Tulsa that night but changed their minds because Daniel was there. They all sat in the kitchen talking. Olivia was still wearing her dress and sat beside her father holding his hand. "The last time I was here, you had a tornado, and now I'm getting a grandchild," he said. "What do you folks do on ordinary days around here?"

Olivia and Bobby and Mary Lily and Crow went to bed early, but Daniel and Little Sun stayed up late, asking each other questions and telling stories.

At dawn, Bobby and Olivia got up and started driving back to work. "When you're gone, I'll make it up to the newspaper," Olivia said. "I know they think I've been

132

goofing off and I have been, but when you're gone, I won't have anything to do but work."

"The blessing was the best thing I've ever known," Bobby said. "Your dad's going to stay with your folks for a few days; then he's coming to stay with us. Is that the deal?"

"I guess so. He's so mellow since he quit drinking. I don't know what he's up to. He's just like his father used to be. My granddaddy. I guess we all revert to type."

Daniel Hand ended up staying in Tahlequah for four days. He and Little Sun rode the countryside in Little Sun's pickup truck. They spent an afternoon riding Arabian horses at Kayo's stables and another afternoon trout fishing and took the trout back to Crow, and she fried them in a black iron skillet and they ate them with corn bread and cooked spinach and carrots.

They explored the headquarters of the Cherokee Nation and watched a film about the Trail of Tears, which made Daniel cry. They talked about horses and fescue and politics and war and found they were on the same side in just about everything.

Bobby was scheduled to leave on January 30, a Sunday. His company was to meet at

5 a.m. to be bused to the airplane. "I may be second in command at a Motor Transport Division," he told her the night before. "That's the latest word anyway. So you don't need to start worrying about me until I call and tell you to worry. The government's not putting any Americans in the line of fire at this point, and by the time I get there, the Iraqi election will be over and things will be cooling down. Look at me. Promise me you won't worry until I tell you it's time."

Olivia stood up and put both her hands on her slightly protruding belly. She held her shoulders back. She felt very beautiful and it showed. "I will be a warrior too," she promised. "Go on, then. Get out of here." She allowed him to caress her; then he picked up his pack and started out the door to the front walk. A man he knew was picking him up to take him to the armory.

"I'll get home for the birth if there is any way," he said.

"I can have a baby by myself if you don't. I'll have so many people around I probably won't be able to think."

"Good-bye."

"I love you." Then he was gone. Olivia walked back to her office and began the editorial for Tuesday's paper.

5
WAR

Weapons Company, Third Battalion, Twenty-fifth Marines, Fourth Marine Division, based in Tulsa, Oklahoma, had twenty-six men from the Cherokee Nation, six Arapahos and nineteen Chickasaws. The rest were men from small towns in the area and of mixed Scotch, English, Irish, German, and Italian stock. There were six Hispanics and four African Americans. There were identical twins from Healing Springs, three members of the 1996 Hogscald football team, and a young man with a missing finger, who had just gone to work as the assistant director of sports news for the University of Tulsa. None of these men were happy about being called back to duty, but only a few were talking about it.

At five in the morning on a bleak, cold, rainy day, it seemed a pretty unhappy-looking group of men, and Bobby Tree wasn't in the mood to try to cheer them up.

"I just got married and my wife's pregnant," he answered the elderly civilian who checked off their names as they boarded the bus that was taking them to the transport plane. "How the hell do you think I feel?"

"Maybe it won't last much longer," the man said. "You never can tell. If the Republicans lose Congress in the next election, this all could change."

"Well, don't tell that to anyone else this morning." Bobby threw back his shoulders and started acting like a soldier. "We got a job to do."

"Whatever," the man answered. "Well, here's the list. Have them sign by their names. You'll be on the plane in an hour and then we're off to the races." The civilian was a retired fireman. He worked weekends at a casino on the Arkansas border, and then on the air base whenever they called him in. He had profited from the war. He'd made five hundred dollars doing part-time work in the past month, and maybe fifteen or sixteen thousand dollars since the thing began. He needed the work and had gotten in the habit of following the war closely on television and in the newspapers. Some days he was glad the United States had declared war on Iraq, and sometimes he was sorry and wished it would hurry up

136

and end.

It was eight in the morning before the company was on the plane to take them to begin their basic training. As soon as everyone was seated and strapped in, Bobby got out his notebook and began his first letter to Olivia.

Dear Olivia,

I don't know what they will let us write, so this may be held up or parts marked out. Since I don't know anything yet, I don't know what I could write that I shouldn't write. Anyway, we are on a transport plane and in a few minutes should be taking off for six weeks of training before we're posted. You can probably fly there before I leave, but they may let me come home if I'm being sent overseas.

It's not bad being with the men. Most of them are acting good, only two really griping, and I'm not in the mood to start yelling at people yet.

When our folks went to war, they knew who they were fighting and what they were protecting or who they were mad at and for what. Men don't have that anymore. We have to trust our leaders. That's what Semper Fi is all about.

That's what the marines are about, trusting the chain of command, so I'm going to do that until I see a reason to stop doing it, and I'm going to do it then too.

I'm a good soldier and I'm proud to be an American. I know you hate that kind of shit, but I don't hate it.

I think about the baby a lot. Let me know as soon as you find out if it's a boy or a girl. I can't help wanting a son, but I don't care.

I love you, baby. Take good care of things there and take care of yourself and the baby, boy or girl. I love what's in there, hidden in you, and made of you and me.

Maybe I'll write a country-and-western song. Send me my guitar. Just kidding.

Love,
Bobby

While Bobby was writing this letter, Olivia was sitting at her desk in the newspaper office, eating a tuna fish sandwich on whole wheat bread and thinking about a poem she had found that morning on the Internet. It contained a metaphor of such power that she had thought of nothing else since she read it, was seeing everything she thought of in the context of the poem.

She called her secretary into the room and gave her a copy of the poem and told her to find out what it would cost to reproduce it in the paper.

"We should be publishing a poem a day," she announced. "I told Jim that was what I wanted ten months ago and then I forgot about it. I'll just start doing it and see if he yells. I want to start with this one. Mary Oliver is a famous poet. It's Beacon Press. Call an editor there and see what they say."

"I like this," the secretary said, looking up from the poem, "but I'm not sure I know what it means."

"It's a metaphor. Think of the bear as this war. Think of it as nature in all its glory and death. Or hell, just read it. I don't want to tell you what it means."

"It's about spring," the secretary said. "It says 'Spring' right here in the title."

"Read it out loud," Olivia said. "Maybe it *is* only about spring. Maybe I'm projecting."

"Read it out loud?"

"Sure. Read it. Indulge me."

The secretary, whose name was Callie Mayfield, and who had been a good student in English classes when she was at the university and would have majored in English, but her father made her go to business school because he thought the humanities were run by a bunch of gooks, stood up and put on her best manner and read the poem out loud.

"Wow," Olivia said. "Where did you learn to read like that?"

"I acted in all the plays in high school. I was Miranda in *The Tempest*. It's on my résumé."

"You're right, it's about spring. It's just with Bobby gone . . ."

"What do you hear?"

"Not much, not yet. He's applying to be a technician on some special ops thing they are doing in Nevada. He takes the tests next week. Say a prayer he gets in. It would keep him in the States."

"I will," Callie said. "I'll say one every day."

Bobby Tree's battalion had been chosen six months earlier to take an aptitude test for training to help drone pilots and sensor operators at a desert base forty-five miles northwest of Las Vegas, Nevada. The air force could not recruit enough technicians for the work, and the Pentagon was lending them men from the marines.

Bobby and two other men from his company had scored high grades on the preliminary tests, and as soon as the company was at its training base, the three men were called in and asked to take a second series of tests. One man was an accountant from Skiatook, Oklahoma. The second man had spent his youth playing computer games at a mall in Tulsa. The third was Bobby Tree, with his innate three-dimensional sense and his fine near vision and the touch that made him Olivia's lifetime greatest lover.

A week after the second round of tests, the three men were called into the office of the base commandant and told where they were going.

"This may not sound like exciting work," the colonel told them. "But every day you will save more lives than you can imagine. Every time a drone does the work of a manned flight, Americans live. There aren't enough pilots, and the air force needs every one they can find. It's a complicated procedure and involves very long hours. Any questions?"

"When do we start?" the accountant asked. His eyes were shining. He was a quiet man who had read adventure novels all his life. Now, at last, a real adventure was being offered to him. A hush-hush, state-of-the-art sort of adventure, out in the desert, where all good secret operations should be carried on.

Bobby said, "I have a wife who's going to have a baby in six months. Will I be able to go home on leave and see her?"

"Not right away," the colonel answered. "No one can know exactly where you are. No e-mails for a while once you're there, although you can write letters that will be read by censors before being mailed. Partly the reason you have been picked is your mental stability. If I were young, I'd give anything to be in on this. I think you're pretty lucky."

"I'm a marine, sir. I go where I'm told. I was just wondering if it meant I might get to be there for the birth."

"I don't know about that."

"Yes, sir. Thank you, sir."

"Dear Olivia," Bobby e-mailed Olivia that night. "I can't tell you much except something good has happened that you would be glad to know. I will not be in danger. So quit worrying about that and tell my dad, and if you don't hear from me for a while, don't worry about anything. Take care of yourself and him or her. I can't help thinking it's a boy, he's a boy, or she's a boy. Okay, I love you. Bobby. I hope you get this."

■ ■ ■ ■

Little Sun was in the pasture, sitting cross-legged on a ceremonial blanket. It was seven in the morning and the sun was just beginning to warm up the edges of the world. He had eaten breakfast at five and gone out to say his prayers to the earth and think of his strong grandson-in-law in a barracks with other men, waiting to know his future and his fate. Little Sun thought also of his great-grandchild in Olivia's womb and of what a strong and brave child it would be, and how it would carry his heart into another hundred years of happenings in the world and perhaps be a great leader for their people or a healer or a dreamer or a man who could talk to horses, as Bobby sometimes seemed able to do and as he knew for sure his friend Kayo could do.

When Olivia received Bobby's e-mail, she read it, printed it, deleted it from her computer, folded the piece of paper, and put it in her shirt pocket. Then she went out of the building to sit on the steps in the sunshine and watch the smokers clustered together under a couple of scraggly-looking pin oak trees growing up through round circles in the thirty-year-old concrete. Above the city of Tulsa the winter skies were gray and blue and full of long white cirrus clouds, more like spring than winter.

I'll figure it out, she decided. I'll call Jack Reed in Oklahoma City and ask him what he thinks. He'll know who to call.

She got up from the steps and walked down the street to a newsstand and bought copies of six newspapers, including the *New York Times* and the *Washington Post* and the *Wall Street Journal.* She could have pulled up the papers' content on her computer, but she wanted to read it the old-fashioned way.

It took her a couple of days to figure out what Bobby was doing. By the time she did, her house was a sea of unwashed dishes, clothes were thrown on the floor, and piles of newspapers were everywhere.

At her office her desk was piled high with more newspapers, her computer was full of unanswered e-mails, and her last three editorials had been boring rehashes of the pope's illness, a school shooting at a reservation in Montana, and a diatribe about secondary school education in Tulsa.

But she had figured it out. There was only one thing going on in the United States armed services that would require that

144

much secrecy and that much intuitive reasoning and mechanical skills: Bobby was being trained to fly drones. He had a commercial pilot's license he had picked up when he worked in Montana as a young man. He understood electronics and machinery.

"If I'm right, they'll be sending him to Nevada," she told her old friend Jack Reed on the telephone. Jack had been calling people he knew in the Defense Department and picking their brains.

"Bingo," Jack said. "If it's true, he's a lucky man and not just because he won't have to go over there and eat sand. That's exciting work."

"Pray for him, Jack," Olivia said. "I need all the help I can get this year."

"We've started praying?"

"We always did. We just didn't call it that."

Dearest Olivia,

I probably won't be able to send this to you, so I'll keep a copy and give it to you when I am able. It's final and I'm excited about this. Not as much as I am about Robert Little Sun Daniel Tree being born or Summer Rivers Tree or whatever we end up naming him, but still I'm plenty excited.

Here's the deal. I leave for Nellis Air Force Base on March 15. They are going to teach me to fly Pioneers and Dragon Eyes. These are drones. If I'm really good at it, they may let me fly Predators and Global Hawks.

I scored a 100 on the aptitude deal they made me take. Arvest Iron Hawk scored better than I did and he's going too. He scored the same as I did, but he did it in a lot less time, the paper part where you draw things. I guess he was good at geometry. Anyway, it looks like the Cherokees are going to have to win them another war. Hell, baby, I'm really happy about this. I wanted to be a pilot the first time around, and Tom McAlphin was always trying to get me to do that, but I was too heartbroken about breaking up with you to be a good enough soldier. I flew Tom's plane all over Montana, with him as a passenger. One time we even took it to Alaska. Well, anyway, now I have this chance, and it might not be the same thing as getting in a fighter jet and pulling nine g's, but what the hell, it's a chance to do something really interesting to help with the war. If they let you have this letter, call Tom and tell him what I'm doing, will you? We should have invited him and Sharrene to the wedding, but I was too busy to remember to do it.

Be happy for me, baby, and for us, because I don't think I'm going to get killed at Nellis Air Force Base, Nevada, but I might be in the middle of some scrabbling between the marines and the air force. The commander of the squadron told me I'd be serving two masters for a while and just to be cool and do the best I could.

Here's some data. I don't think they mind if I tell you this because it's been in the *New York Times* and all those papers up there.

There are three existing Predator squadrons in the air force and they are adding fifteen more. There are also squadrons in the marines and the army, but they are in such a pinch for pilots that they are just training everyone at the same place for the next six months to a year. I might end up at a marine base teaching other people. Anything can happen this year, I guess, and I hate to say it, but this war is making opportunities for men and women too. Although I haven't seen any women doing it yet, I heard they were.

I guess it would be good work for queers when they let them back in. I know you don't like to hear that, but hell, I like queers. I like your queer friends in Tulsa a lot, and one of your cousins in North Carolina is a queer and I can't believe none of you know it. He's a great guy. He was my favorite of all the ones who went hunting with your dad and me.

So I guess you're thinking, What is Bobby smoking? Well, you've made me so happy, and now this. I need to go run three miles and get this out of me. I love you, baby. I think I'll get to see you for a day or two before I head out for Nevada. Maybe you can meet me there.

Love again,
Love always,
Bobby

The letter arrived on March 20, by which time Bobby had told her most of it on the phone and by which time the sonogram had confirmed that the baby was a boy.

"Bobby's coming on Thursday," Olivia told her friends at the newspaper. "I want everything for the paper to be set before he gets here. All we have to do is make sure we have the pope's sickness covered and make sure my editorials will fit and then you guys have to take over here for two days. You can't take this away from me."

"We got it covered," her secretary and the assistant editors assured her. "Unless there's a terrorist attack, we can do the rest."

"What did he say when he found out it was a boy?" her arts editor asked. "I've been waiting to hear about that."

"I haven't told him. I want to tell him to his face."

"To his face" happened on March 31 at two in the afternoon when Bobby got off a Northwest Airlines flight and walked into the lobby of the Tulsa Airport, wearing his uniform and looking like all the goodness and holiness of the world, and Olivia took him in her arms and told him her news as soon as she kissed him.

"I know you wanted a son," she said. "And I've got you one."

"Don't be mad at me for wanting one," he said. "I have to fix up all that bad stuff with my dad."

"So what exactly will you do?" she asked him in the car on the way home from the airport. He was driving. She was sitting as close to him as she could, touching the

149

sleeve of his jacket.

"I sit in a simulated cockpit sort of thing and fly the drone, and in Iraq there are soldiers on the ground telling me what they need it to do. The things can see like eagles. They can corner. They can get into tight places — at least the small ones can. They can launch missiles or small bombs or large bombs, and they can watch the back of a building or scope out warm spaces in pavement. The insurgents set asphalt on fire so they can dig it up quickly to put bombs or explosives under it. It stays warm for quite a while. Sensors on the drones can sense the differences in temperature of pavement or even the newness of pieces of pavement. There's a lot of chemistry I have to learn. It's not just playing with the controls, although that's the main thing. It's touch, baby, just like making love." He put his hand on her leg and ran it up her thigh to her crotch. "Goddamn, I'm horny. Is it going to hurt him if we screw? I've been worrying about that."

"Well, you can't get kinky."

"When did we ever need that?"

"Never. I was just kidding. I'm too happy to be serious right now. I've got enough of that going on at work. I'm thinking about quitting my job. I mean it. It's too much shit going on while I'm worrying about you and making this baby. What if the baby finds out all the shit I have to know to run the paper?"

"Then he'll know the world and won't have to find out the hard way."

The following afternoon they decided on the spur of the moment to go to Tahlequah. They arrived at three, and Little Sun took Bobby off with him to the meadow. "I don't matter to Granddaddy anymore," Olivia said. "He doesn't even try to talk to me. I think all he wanted me for was to get Bobby back into the family."

"I am making you some blankets," Mary Lily said. "Come in your old room and look at what I'm weaving for the baby."

Bobby Tree and Little Sun were sitting cross-legged in front of the earth island, watching the sun go down. They had not spoken in many minutes.

"So you attack the enemy from ambush," Little Sun said at last. "I do not think there is any shame in that. If he is the enemy of your people."

"It's hard work," Bobby answered. "Many hours a day. We don't have enough men to do it. Every time we use one of these

151

unmanned planes, we save the lives of American soldiers."

"Then do a good job of it. Be the best of the ones who do it. Then you will be proud."

"I never was a coward. I've never been afraid."

"Stop worrying about it and do the job they give you. Olivia is very happy that you will be in Nevada."

"Will you bless me then, Grandfather?"

"I will." Little Sun got up and went to the earth island. He took a handful of dirt and broke it up in his hand and came back to Bobby and said prayers of blessing and then put the earth onto his cheeks and arms and gave him some to hold in his hand.

Little Sun sat back down on his blanket, and the two men watched the sun until it was far down below the horizon and the red and purple and golden light had faded into the dark cold blue of evening.

Later that night Olivia and Bobby drove back to Tulsa.

Then it was Sunday and then it was Monday, and on Tuesday morning at 4 a.m., Bobby got up from their bed and put on his uniform and left. "I won't be far away," he said. "Stay warm. Take care of my son." Then he was gone and the long spring and summer lay ahead of Olivia, and although she didn't have to think every minute of every day that he would be killed, she had to soldier on without his presence.

"Which I've done most of my adult life," she said out loud as she pulled the sheets up on the bed and tossed the pillows against the headboard and headed out to run a newspaper, when there was no news to report except who had been invited to accompany the president to Rome to the funeral of the pope, and who had not been invited, and which women had perhaps chosen not to go because the pope represented everything women in the contemporary world were fighting to leave behind. "Family values," Olivia muttered to herself as she drove into the parking lot behind the newspaper office. "Now I'm talking to myself. That's nice. Maybe I ought to go see my old psychiatrist. I wonder what she's up to lately."

It was 7 a.m. when Olivia sat down at her desk and began to attack the papers in front of her. It was 11 a.m. before she started reading the e-mails. It was after lunch before she started sorting out the letters to the editor that had already been screened by one of her favorite junior editors, a recent graduate of Oklahoma State whom

Olivia was grooming to be the living-section editor.

"Dear Editor," one letter began. "What in the shit do those people in Washington think they're doing? They don't do a goddamn thing all day but think about how to get elected again. This Terri Schiavo thing is the last goddamn straw. I pay taxes to pay the salaries of these whores and I mean both Democrat and Republican. I've had it. The only government I like is *The West Wing* and I'm not sure about what will happen when President Bartlet is gone. The ones coming up there are as bad as the ones we really have. April fool. Your cousin Tallulah, lost in Nashville in the rain. I have decided to become a writer like you. I'm starting out with letters to editors signed with pseudonyms. What do you think?"

"Dear Tallulah," Olivia e-mailed her back. "Letters to editors are the perfect place for you to start. You'll have to watch the hard language, however. What will your pseudonym be?"

" 'Lost in Nashville' is a possibility," Tallulah e-mailed back. " 'Tired of Whores' is a contender. 'Keeping My Eye on the Ball' is another. I'm not finished deciding this yet. I only decided on my new career this morning. It was raining and the indoor courts are leaking."

"It's an imperfect world," Olivia e-mailed her back. "Roofs leak and machines break. Love, Busy in Tulsa. Ten four."

On April 8, 2005, at 9:45 a.m., Bobby Tree sat down at a simulated cockpit and dropped the first bomb on a village. At 9:57 he launched a rocket that described an arc that landed on a bunker, took aerial photographs of a ten-mile section of land to the north of Baghdad, and flew back to a landing strip in the desert near Syria.

When he stopped for lunch, he was drenched with sweat. "Goddamn," he told a friend. "This is work."

Olivia was sitting in her office, eating rye crackers and soy cheese and vegetable chips. She was drinking ginger tea from a Yoga Studio cup so old it had begun to look like raku pottery. She studied the lines on the cup, the beautiful cracks that led everywhere and nowhere, and she thought about the years she had spent doing yoga with the woman who had given her the cup, who had died seven months ago from an aggressive lung cancer that had attacked and spread thirteen years after she quit smoking. Yin and yang, Olivia decided. And what in the hell am I doing this far away from Bobby when the United States of America is at war and all my writing and yelling couldn't get 1 percent more citizens of the state of Oklahoma to cast a vote in a presidential election. There are bigger fish to fry than selling advertising for Jim's newspaper.

Olivia was in a slump because the publishers had refused to print an editorial about the war, saying the editorial was too biased in favor of the administration.

I quit, Olivia decided. I used to like this job. Now I hate it. I don't know why I ever took this job, and I don't like to sit behind this desk on the first really beautiful sunny spring day in a week. It's unhealthy for my baby to breathe this air. I need to get out where the air is better than this. I want to go to Tahlequah and see Granddaddy and Grandmother.

She picked up some notes on a yellow legal pad and studied them. Then she began to type on the old-fashioned typewriter she kept on a stand in her office. It had belonged to her aunt Anna. It was the last typewriter Anna had used before she died. It was the typewriter Anna used to write *Prime Numbers* and *Binding Energy.*

The Tulsa World
315 South Boulder Avenue
Tulsa, Oklahoma
Office of the Editor in Chief

Dear Sir or Madam,

I am the editor of the *Tulsa World* and I have been a supporter of President Bush since 2001. My editorials for the last three years will attest to that support.

My husband is a staff sergeant in the marine reserves. He is Bobby Tree, a member of Twenty-fifth Marines, Fourth Marine Division, Oklahoma.

His company was called to active duty in December 2004, and he reported for duty to Camp Pendleton on January 30, 2005.

He has been assigned to duty in a pilot training program at Nellis Air Force Base, Nevada, effective April 5, 2005.

My résumé is enclosed. I would like to volunteer for duty in any post near Nellis Air Force Base for the duration of the campaign in Iraq. I speak French and Spanish well, if not fluently, and am a quick study in languages. My real skills, however, would be as a publicist or lobbyist for the Predator and other drone aircraft systems.

I understand engineering concepts and mechanical devices and can explain such things in clear, cogent English.

I would be willing to take a prolonged leave of absence from my job as editor of this newspaper to be available for whatever work you could find for me. I would be glad to go to Washington, D.C., to do lobbying there, or to fly anywhere to talk to senators or representatives or groups of concerned or interested citizens.

I am three months pregnant, but my aunt, a full-blooded Cherokee Indian, who speaks six Indian dialects, including Navajo, and whose résumé I also include, will come to live with me as long as my husband is on active duty. She will help me care for my child, should I be fortunate enough to get to work for you.

My main aim, of course, is to live nearer to my husband during this time in our lives, but I am also committed to helping the cause that he serves and in which we both believe.

Yours most sincerely,
Olivia de Havilland Hand Tree

I should have used the computer, Olivia

decided as she got up from the desk and began to search around for a box of envelopes.

"Callie," she called to her secretary, "I need you."

"What?" The girl stood in the door grinning. "I heard you in here typing. What do you need? A stamp?"

"Copy this on the computer and send it to the Pentagon in Washington, would you?"

"Sure thing, boss." The girl took the letter and read it. "You can't mean this?"

"I've already told Jim I'm doing it. Send a copy to my husband, while you're at it. Well, I have to get to work."

Olivia left the typewriter and began pulling up her e-mails. There were forty messages. She read and answered a few, then switched to a program that had ticker tape news from Iraq. "Thirteen men killed, many wounded, in attack on training base for Iraqi police. Six Americans among the dead. All members of Cherokee Company."

She knew about the deaths hours before Bobby knew. He was at a console, practicing liftoffs for a fourteen-foot reconnaissance drone called the Pioneer. He had lifted off the imaginary plane nineteen times and reread the manual twice, then gotten up and decided to walk up and down the hallway outside the console cluster to stretch his legs. Most of the pilots exercised in the early morning and again at night. The most ambitious ones also did stretches and fast walks or quick runs during their breaks.

He walked out into the hall and read the streaming news banner that ran 24-7 across the far hall doorways. There it was, the fate he had escaped by being in Nevada. He was crying when he came back to the console, tears of guilt and rage. This is war, he kept thinking. What in the hell did I think I was doing? How old am I? Who were they? There's no way I'll have names until late tonight. I can't call the battalion. I have to sit here at this desk and play with this toy airplane and that's that. That's what's going on. Olivia knows by now. She might know who it is.

"I need to make a telephone call," he told the captain in charge of the console cluster. "Six members of my company were killed in Iraq this morning. I need to know who they are, sir. May I make the call, sir?"

"Let me help you, Sergeant. Come in my office." The tall captain led the way into an office and closed the door.

"Let's turn on my computer," he said. "Sit down. That's tough, soldier. That's tough."

■ ■ ■ ■

It was one of the twins from Tennessee. It was a close friend of Bobby's named Trent and an older man named John Little and two men from Tulsa and two from Tahlequah.

"I'm married to the newspaper editor in Tulsa, Oklahoma," Bobby said. "Sir, may I call and find out what she knows?"

"Go ahead. Then go back to work, Sergeant."

"Thank you, sir. I will, sir. I won't talk long."

"She isn't here," Olivia's secretary told him. "You can try her cell, but I think she left it here. Yeah, it's on the desk. She went out with a reporter to talk to the parents of the men from Tulsa. She ought to be back soon. Can she call you?"

"I don't think so. Tell her I know. I'll talk to her tonight. Tell her I'm okay. It's war, Callie. I had forgotten this was a war."

"We all had," Callie said. "Only now I won't. The town will be in mourning. The town cares. Tulsa cares."

"I have to go to work."

"Do a good job. I'll find her and let

161

her know."

Callie Mayfield looked down at her fingernails. It had been three weeks since she had last bitten them, and they were beginning to look normal. She started to raise her right hand to her mouth; then she stuck it behind her and marched to her desk and got out the bottle of thick black liquid and painted it all over both sets of fingernails. I hate being a baby biting my nails, she thought, when all I have to do all day is get up and get dressed and come in here and work for the best boss I ever had. If she leaves, I'm going with her. I'm going wherever she goes. Maybe I'll enlist. I could fly those planes too. I used to be real good at video games, real, real good. I used to beat my brothers; well, not often, but sometimes I did.

Olivia was sitting on the sofa in a small, clean room, holding the hand of a mother who had just learned her twenty-nine-year-old only son had died and was not coming back to Tulsa, Oklahoma, ever. He had never married and had no children. There would be no one to fix things for her when they were broken, no one to call her on Mother's Day or love her when she was old or be there in the world or hold her hand when she died. Gone. Gone forever, never, never, never to return.

"Your sister's on her way from Broken Arrow," Olivia was saying. "She'll be here soon."

"Okay," the woman said. "Thank you for finding her. Okay. Thank you for coming here."

The reporter who had accompanied Olivia walked across the room from where he had been interviewing a neighbor who had come to help. "Your husband called from Nevada," he told Olivia. "He said he knew about it. Callie said you can't call back."

The woman tightened her grip on Olivia's hand. She was breathing so slowly that Olivia wasn't sure she was breathing at all. "Get a doctor over here," Olivia said to the reporter. "Call Roger Montrose and ask him if he can come by after work. He's Cherokee. He'll come."

"Okay," the reporter said.

"Okay," the woman on the sofa said, and loosened her grip on Olivia's hand a small bit. She seemed to actually take a breath of air.

"Open the front door," Olivia said. "Get some air in here."

It was several more hours before Olivia and the reporter got to the second house.

This one was better. There was a large family and they were gathering. There was food, a long table laden with things the neighbors had brought to eat: sliced turkey and ham, rice casserole, a platter of broiled peppers and asparagus and kale, potato salad with scallions and homemade mayonnaise. When she saw the table, Olivia realized she hadn't eaten in hours. She fixed herself a plate of food and sat on a chair at a card table and ate the food slowly and carefully, with thankfulness for the kindness that had brought it there. She was joined at the table by a middle-aged couple, and she talked to them without interviewing them or thinking of using anything they told her in an editorial or a story.

The reporter who had accompanied her came and stood by the table and asked Olivia if there was anything she needed. She borrowed his telephone and called her office and talked to her secretary. "What did he say?"

"That he'd try to call you tonight. He said it is a war. That he'd just realized this was a war."

"Stay until I get back. You're going to have to stay late tonight."

"Okay. That's okay."

■ ■ ■ ■

Callie looked down at her nails. The stuff was wearing off. She pulled open her desk drawer and took out the bottle and angrily painted all the nails again. Then she sat down at her desk and started going through the e-mails.

At four that afternoon, Olivia got back to her office and went to work. She had a meeting with her editorial staff and arranged more meetings for the morning. Then she went to work on an editorial for the morning's paper. It wasn't everything she wanted to say or thought needed saying, but it was a beginning. A CAUTIOUS OPTIMISM was the headline, although KNOWING I DON'T KNOW WHAT WE SHOULD DO NEXT would have been even more honest.

"And we are here as on a darkling plain
Swept with confused alarms of struggle
   and flight,
Where ignorant armies clash by night."

And clash and clash and clash and have clashed and will clash.

I am a pregnant woman whose husband has been called up to active duty but has not yet been sent into the war, where three days ago six men of Cherokee Company of the United States Marine Corps were killed in action, leaving broken hearts and grieving families all over our part of the United States of America.

"And tell the pleasant prince this mock of
   his
Hath turn'd his [tennis] balls to gun-stones,
   and his soul
Shall stand sore charged for the wasteful
   vengeance
That shall fly with them; for many a thou-
   sand widows
Shall this his mock mock out of their dear
   husbands;
Mock mothers from their sons, mock
   castles down;
And some are yet ungotten and unborn
That shall have cause to curse the Dau-
   phin's scorn.
But this lies all within the will of God,
To whom I do appeal, and in whose name
Tell you the Dauphin I am coming on
To venge me as I may, and to put forth
My rightful hand in a well-hallow'd cause.
So get you hence in peace; and tell the

Dauphin
His jest will savor but of shallow wit,
When thousands weep more than did
    laugh at it. —
Convey them with safe conduct. — Fare
    you well."
                    — William Shakespeare

"A wasteful vengeance," is that what we are doing here? I do not think so. I believe we were attacked and are now mounting a long and costly counterattack that will not end for many years, maybe for my lifetime.

I am proud that my husband has gone to serve his country. I grieve for the families of the fallen. I pray to God that we find ways to protect ourselves that do not require the lives and limbs of our sons and daughters.

Here at the *Tulsa World* we are opening our letters columns to all of you. I don't believe our readers are sitting quietly out there, speechless and undetermined, or worse, uncaring. I think you are as confused as I am by all of this. Talking about it and writing about it and sharing our opinions will help us to think clearly.

We will print letters with the names withheld if you do not want to sign your letters.

Tell us what you think.

Also, we are going to devote one column every day to detailed explanations of which troops are in Iraq and Afghanistan, what weapons they are using, where the weapons are being manufactured, within the limits of national security, and we are going to conduct several public hearings about the war.

We are at war. The deaths this week have brought this home to us. Pray for the families of the lost, and for all of us everywhere.

When she had finished the editorial, she stood up and patted her stomach. The ungotten and unborn, she decided. The future.

She walked out of her office and down a hall to the office of her old friend Big Jim Walters and handed him the editorial. "I'm going outside to walk a few blocks and then I'll be back. I won't be gone long. Can you read it now?"

"Don't go out on the street by yourself this time of day. Take someone with you."

"I need to think. Sam will be back with the stories about the families soon. I want to go over all that before I leave tonight. I don't think we can get it ready for tomorrow. Let's do it the day after."

"Fine with me. Well, let me read."

Olivia left the building and stepped out onto the wide sidewalks that surrounded the building. She breathed in a long, deep breath of city air and began to walk. I need to think about this baby. I need to take better care of myself and I will, starting now. I'll get to bed by ten or eleven. I'm fine. Nothing's wrong. I'm strong as a horse except I worry all the time. Oh, God, I forgot: Bobby might call back.

She checked to make sure her cell phone was in the side pocket of her beige Banana Republic carpenter pants, which still fit if she left the waistband undone. Then she started walking fast, trying to remember to breathe like a yogi. The real world is tough as nails, she decided. Tough as hell, tough the way nature is tough, relentless, coming at you below the knees just when you think you're safe. You're never safe. But at least I mostly think I'm safe. I have a gift for thinking things will turn out okay, only that's not enough anymore. I've got to start thinking like a warrior. We aren't safe, but we can fight for our children and for one another; we can protect our tribe, whatever we perceive that to be. And I don't get to quit the newspaper or quit a damn thing. Hell, maybe I ought to get Mary Lily to come live with me for a while, although she'd go crazy locked up in a house in Tulsa.

She had gone three blocks, circumnavigating the one on which the newspaper building sat, when the phone rang. She leaned against a wall and took the call.

"What can we do?" Bobby said. "They're gone, and if I'd been there I'd be dead too. It was a convoy with all hands. I'd have been with them."

"How does that make you feel?"

"Like I don't know what to feel. I'm glad I'm not there, and I'm glad I'm not dead, and I don't feel like I want to kill everyone over there to get revenge. I thought I would feel that way, but I don't. What I'm doing is very precise, Olivia. Precise information, precise attacks — that's what I like about it. You wouldn't believe how sensitive these drones are, even the big ones, but I'm only working on a small one that belongs to the marines. They said I'm going to get to learn to fly the Predators too before I leave. It's so precise. It's like an operation. Everyone who's here — the teachers, the older pilots — is very businesslike. It's a long way from what our ancestors thought of as war."

"Is that good?"

"The end result is still blown-up buildings and dead people. But fewer dead innocents,

I guess. I hope and pray."

"Okay. When are they going to let me see you?"

"Maybe in six weeks. They won't say. Everything is a secret. Where are you?"

"Walking around the block. It's nice here. Beautiful low clouds, a great sunset; the storms last week cleaned up the place, so the pollen isn't bad. Lots of fat people. People starting to say bad things about the pope after two weeks of sucking up. It's Oklahoma in the spring. What can I say?"

"How's my son? Is he moving around yet?"

"No, but he's in there. I'm going home soon. I'm going to bed early. We went to see the families of the men from Tulsa. It was bad."

"You want to tell me about it?"

"No. I have to get back to the office. I love you, Bobby. I'll call you later if I can."

"You can't, but I'll try to call you. Over and out."

"Hanging up."

Olivia finished the block she was on, then speeded up and walked back to the entrance to the building and went inside. She took the elevator to her floor and went into her office, where she got to work putting out the newspaper.

Jim handed the editorial back to her with three changes. "We don't print anonymous letters," he said.

"I know it," she answered. "I was just floating that."

"We can't do it."

"I know it. I got carried away."

Little Sun had gone to the earth island to think and smoke. Crow knew he still smoked and sometimes even let him do it in the house, but he didn't like to do it around her because it made him feel bad.

He sat down cross-legged on his blanket and lit his pipe and inhaled deeply; then he watched the sun go down. He knew about the deaths in Iraq. He knew how bad it would make Bobby feel. He put it out of his mind and thought about good things that were happening. His son Roper was going to be a grandfather again. His son Creek had bought another piece of land on the river and was planning on building a house there. His daughter Xanthe was going to marry the man she had been living with for seven months. She was forty-six years old and wanted to have a baby. If she was crazy enough to have a baby when she was old enough to be its grandmother, it was okay with Little Sun. He had been watching the world for seventy-five years. Nothing surprised him anymore and nothing bothered him as much as it used to.

Tuesday, April 12, 2005. Dawn came with the sound of mockingbirds in the oak trees above Olivia's bedroom windows. A nest of baby birds were learning to fly in the high branches. The racket they made had begun to wake her every morning at five thirty. Above the trees a brightening sky stood out against the new leaves, and everything in the world was charged with life and procreative power and hunger and flight.

The world is full of hunger, Olivia thought. And I am part of all the world, of trees and plants and birds and song and flight and hunger and the hunt, of war and the surcease of war.

U.S. COMMANDERS SEE A REDUCTION OF TROOPS IN IRAQ, was the headline for the morning's paper. Olivia had heard the carrier land a paper on her front doorstep about the time the birds had woken her.

I cannot leave the newspaper, she decided. I am in a place to influence more people in more ways than any job I could do in Washington. I can go to Nevada and write a story without having to get permission from some general at the Pentagon. The same people will decide what's classified one way or the other.

Oh, God, could you please let me wake one morning thinking of something but the goddamn war. I think we had to fight this war, and if I'm wrong, at least I have skin in the game.

I am thirty-six years old, almost thirty-seven, and I am pregnant. Think of that, for Christ's sake. Half the people my age can't have a baby because they waited too long and took too many birth control pills and fucked up their eggs with all the shit we have pumped into the water and food and earth and air in order to make a more perfect union and a place to live forever with arthritis. That's good, Olivia, she told herself, now you're cooking, now you're thinking like a journalist. Always look for the darkest cloud, find someone to blame, something to mindfuck about.

She got out of bed, took some vitamins, ate breakfast, threw on some clothes, got into the Nissan, and drove down to the paper. She parked in her parking space, locked the car, went into the building, and got to work.

It's my personality, she decided. To hell with it. I can't get a brain transplant.

■ ■ ■ ■

There was an e-mail from Bobby.

"Today I am going to learn to launch small missiles from a plane the size of your granddaddy's living room. Tomorrow I learn to launch them from one the size of our house. In the late afternoons I've volunteered to teach riding to kids at the base. They have some killer horses in this part of the country, but they aren't very well trained. It's good to see horses again. I was out there yesterday from four until seven and the kids are great. I might start wanting to give our son a real Indian name, Sequoyah maybe. What do you think?"

Dear Bobby,

I think I'm the luckiest woman in the world to have you. Get the war over and get your ass on home and into my bed. I dreamed about fucking you all night. It was so weird because our kid was sleeping in a bed in the same room and the only time we could fuck was when he was taking a bath, but when he finally got in the tub, you fell asleep and then some of my aunts came into the room and sat on the bed and started talking.

175

Then I realized I had on this leather strap that covered up my pussy and I had to take it off under the covers so they wouldn't see what we were doing, and in the end I woke up and we still hadn't fucked each other.

What do you think this dream means?

Love,
Olivia

Dear Olivia,

I hope your computer is more secure than the one we have here.

Love,
Bobby

At eight o'clock that night, Little Sun called Olivia on the telephone. "Mary Lily wants to come stay with you for a while," he said. "She wants to visit the museums there and see if they will lend things to our museum for the powwow next fall."

"No, she doesn't. She's a mind reader and she knows I was thinking about her yesterday and thinking I could get her to come stay with me and calm me down."

"We will be there tomorrow afternoon at five o'clock. Your grandmother and I will drive her there."

"You can't drive at night. Does that mean

you will spend the night away from home?"

"If we do not drive her, Kayo's nephew might bring her in his truck. He may deliver a horse to a man there. I said, 'We have to call Olivia before you leave for her house.' "

"Tell her I want her here very much. Send me some of grandmother's Wagoner stew if she has any made."

"I will tell her. I think you will be strong in these adversities, Granddaughter."

"I'll be strong and smart, Granddaddy. Smart makes me strong."

"Chaz's wife, Rose Little Thunder, will have a baby a month after you have one. We are rich with children now."

"I'm happy for that. Thank you for calling me with all this good news."

"Hang up now and go to bed."

"I will."

Olivia wandered into her bedroom and put on her old flannel pajamas and got into her bed and sat propped up against the head-board, writing on a yellow legal pad, putting together a plan.

Stop worrying, she wrote. Breathe deep yogi breaths for five minutes, morning and night. Take yoga for expectant mothers if I can find time. Get room ready for Mary Lily. Ask Jim if I can do a piece on Nellis

Air Force Base. Keep all appointments at the doctor no matter what happens. Be a good person. Think about my fellow men and fellow women. Expand my universe of sympathy if possible. Don't be a perfectionist. Wear light colors to cheer people up. Don't let Mary Lily stay too long — it will make her sick and drive me crazy.

What else? Live in the present, except that's easier said than done.

Olivia fell asleep with the pencil in her hand and the light on. Twenty minutes later she woke long enough to turn off the light. In the nest above her window the tiny mockingbirds were shoving one another around, growing and getting ready for the morning's flights.

Six o'clock on a Sunday morning. Bells from a chapel a few blocks away were chiming a sweet song. The mockingbirds were in full morning song outside Olivia's bedroom window. The rain and storms of the past week had left the city as clean as a desert isle. Olivia woke and decided not to think so much for a change. She got out of bed, dressed, made a cup of tea, and drank a few sips of it, then walked out of the house and got into her car and went to work. The church bells were still ringing. Is it Mother's

Day? Olivia wondered. Don't turn on the radio, she told herself. Wait till you get to the office.

Just drive the car through the clean streets of the good, safe city where I live. Just go to work. Work is my church, work is my savior, work that is valuable and that adds to the store of knowledge and sometimes goodness, work that informs and teaches and tries to tell the truth. What did Judge Arnold name his book? *Unequal Laws Unto a Savage Race*? It's a line from a poem by Tennyson about Ulysses in his old age, after he gets home to Ithaca. "I mete and dole / Unequal laws unto a savage race." Well, I mete and dole good and bad news unto a careless race, but I do it and I have to keep on doing it even if the Pentagon writes me back and says I can go to work for them. Jim said he didn't even bother to file my letter; he knew I'd change my mind. What a big, fat, smart doll he is. He doesn't have to work. He doesn't have to publish this newspaper. He's got enough dough to live in paradise the rest of his life, and still he gets up every day and works to make the world a better place.

Drive the car, Olivia. Don't think so much. It's Sunday. There's work to do.

6
NELLIS AIR FORCE BASE, NEVADA

On April 1, 2005, Lieutenant Brian Kane, Second Marine Expeditionary Force, Purple Heart recipient with four pieces of titanium and two of plastic in his chin to prove it and two large pieces of his ass now turning into facial skin that would never have to be shaved but wasn't looking bad (although he was considering letting them work on the scars sometime in what he called the distant future), walked out of Walter Reed Army Medical Center in Washington, D.C., and got into the automobile of his late first cousin's fiancée and was driven to her apartment, where he took off his uniform and his medals and got laid for the first time in what seemed like years but had only been a number of months.

For Winifred Hand Abadie, the wait had been even longer, and she was worried that her triweekly vibrator routine had ruined her forever for the real thing. She didn't mention that fear, however, as she turned down the bed with the new 450-count percale sheets rinsed in lavender and took off all her clothes without moving her feet except to kick off her panties. "It's hard to make me come," she said. "So don't worry about it. Just pretend we're in a garage at twilight while our friends play kick the can, so we have to be in a hurry and get in whatever we can."

"That's your fantasy?"

"It is today. I should have opened wine, I guess, or at least made you some tea."

Brian looked down at her body, and his heart rose with his dick. He walked over to Winifred and kissed her very, very gently and lay her down upon her nine-hundred-dollar mattress and her three-hundred-dollar sheets and began to make love to her. He didn't have to try or think or worry; all he had to do was fuck this woman, and he did it.

"This definitely feels better than anything in the whole world," she told him later, when they woke from a nap and lay holding hands. "No one can know what it's like or even remember it, except when it's happening."

"It might not always be this good."

"And then again it might."

"I'm going to Nellis Air Force Base in Nevada in two weeks. I'm going to be assigned to a joint marine–air force group that monitors the satellites that run the Predators and the Global Hawks and all the smaller drones. I want you with me. I want you to marry me as fast as we can, and I want you to go with me to Nevada. Wait a minute." He got out of the bed and went to his clothes and searched in a pocket and found the ring his sister-in-law, Louise, had picked out for him at a jewelry store. He had thrown the box away and put the ring into an envelope and put it in his breast pocket. He pulled it out of the envelope and walked over to the bed and knelt by the bed and held it out to her. "If you don't like it, I'll get you a bigger one."

She sat up in the bed and stuck out her ring finger. "You're supposed to put it on my finger."

"So will you, well, marry me?"

"I will, and the ring's wonderful."

"Louise and Carl went and got it."

"I figured that. Hey, lie back down and get over here close to me and tell me stuff like you are always going to be faithful to me and we'll be able to live on your salary until I get a job and so forth. Come here."

"I've got some money besides my salary.

Pretty much, I think."

"Are you hungry?"

"So much I can't say it."

"I think I'll fix you something to eat. You better try out my cooking."

"I'm sort of sick of eating in bed."

"Then get up and put on that bathrobe in your suitcase and meet me at the dining room table in fifteen minutes."

Winifred went into the kitchen and warmed up a meat loaf she had made the day before and whipped up mashed potatoes with chives. She pulled a wild rice salad out of the refrigerator and added fresh red and yellow bell peppers to it and stuck a loaf of buttered French bread into the oven and then set the table. Seeing she still had two minutes before the fifteen were up, she called her mother and told her she was engaged and hung up without giving her the details. Then she called her cousin Louise and told her she loved the ring. "And call Olivia and tell her Brian is going to Nellis Air Force Base, where Bobby is, and I'm going too. Good-bye. I have to go."

She had finished putting the food and plates on the table when Brian came into the room, holding a book he had found and was reading. "Is this your aunt's book?" he asked.

"One of many. Do you like it?"

"It's beautiful writing. It sounds like you."

"We're all pretty influenced one way or the other. She killed herself because she didn't want to be treated for cancer."

"That's a shame."

"Don't think about it. Come sit at this table and show me your table manners and don't turn your nose up because it's meat loaf. It's made from prime roast and it has pork in it. It's delicious, if I may say so, and it's one of my specialties."

He picked up a fork and cut a piece of the meat loaf and began to eat the first bites of food the woman he was going to marry had ever given him.

"This is worth the skin off my butt," he said. "There were days when I didn't think anything would be worth that. That hurt worse than the goddamn chin."

She held out the ring, looking at it in the light from the candles. She thought for one small moment about the man this man had replaced in her heart, and then she moved the thought to her unconscious mind and lived in the pure joy of the present.

"How will we get married?" she asked. "What do you suggest?"

"I already called and found out what to do. We can do it at the base, or we can get the chaplain who married Carl and Louise. I already called him. He said we should get a license and come on over."

"We have to tell my parents and your parents."

"No, we don't. We've seen more of our parents in the past year than most married people see of theirs in a decade. I mean, if it's up to me, I just want to get a license and do it, well, tomorrow."

"How about Sunday in the Episcopal church, if I can get it going? With our folks and Louise and Carl and maybe a few other people? You ought to invite Dr. Walken, given all you've been through with him. He loves you."

"That's why I wanted it in the hospital. There're a lot of people there I'd like to ask. Well, there we go. Now it's going to be some big deal."

"We must *think on this,*" Winifred declared in her best Shakespearean voice. "*It must be thought upon.* How's your meat loaf?"

"The best I've ever tasted. Come here to me." She went around the table and sat on his lap while he finished eating, and then they went back to bed and made love again and slept and then got up and went around being high on endorphins until Brian remembered he needed to take Advil and a low-dose cortisone pill, and that spoiled the evening for a while.

At nine Monday morning they were down at the Human Resources and Services Department of the Pentagon, being speed-processed into a marriage license and a waived waiting period, and at five that afternoon they stood up before a marine chaplain in a small chapel at the Pentagon and were married. Their only attendants were the secretaries in a nearby office and two officers who were in charge of "event resources."

Winifred was wearing a red silk sheath with a darker red bouclé jacket and three-inch red silk high-heeled sandals, and Brian was wearing his dress uniform. One of the secretaries took photographs with a digital camera and e-mailed them to a list Winifred left with her. There was a message with the photographs: "The couple is expecting guests from two to six on Sunday afternoon at their apartment on D Street. Bring gifts, don't get mad, and be happy for us."

After the ceremony they walked around the city for a while and then went out to dinner and then went home and went to bed. "I think I've been married to you for years," Winifred said. "For twenty years my mother was the best wife and mother on the planet earth. Then she had a relapse, but in the end she went back to my daddy. I'll try to break her record."

"If you have a relapse, I'll shoot the bastard," Brian said. "So don't plan on having one."

On April 13, 2005, Brian flew to Nellis Air Force Base to begin his training. Three days later, Winifred drove to Nevada in a brand-new Ford Explorer packed to the gills with clothes and bedding and household supplies. Someone had rented them an apartment near the base; it was time to start a life.

"What will you do?" Louise asked Winifred. "Are you going to work?"

"Not for a while. I'll play tennis and do Pilates and cook dinner for my husband. I don't know how long he'll be there. They might send him back over."

"They haven't sent Carl yet. It's all changing, Winifred. The midterm elections are coming up. The Republicans aren't going to risk letting Americans get killed, right now anyway."

"I hope to God the decisions aren't based on that."

"Of course they are. That's how the world is done, sweet Cousin. Ask Olivia if you don't believe me. Is she going out there too?"

"She said she'd come for a few days as soon as I got settled. She's running a newspaper. She can't just leave any time she wants to. She can hardly get away at all. She told me she flies out sometimes at ten at night and goes back the next day."

Winifred hung up the phone and went to work unpacking boxes in the small, clean two-bedroom condominium that was their new home. She had packed the minimum necessities for running a house, and she liked what she had chosen. There weren't many things, but they were her favorites: her favorite dish towels; her favorite unbreakable white china; four sets of Gorham Chantilly silver, which had belonged to her grandmother; a new eight-pack of water glasses from the spring Martha Stewart collection at a Kmart she had passed on the road when she was driving; four sets of percale sheets with extra pillowcases, which she had bought when she was in Italy.

"We're camping out," she told people. "I'm leaving things behind like the pioneers

188

did." She made up the bed in the guest room and found a place to hide the lightweight Oreck vacuum her mother had stuffed in her car. "I could buy one there," she had argued.

"But Julia Leigh has a dealership. Why should you pay full price?" Her mother had hoisted the box into the backseat and laid it down on a stack of coats.

Winifred finished the bedrooms, threw the boxes onto the back porch, made notes for colors she wanted to paint the bathrooms, and then wandered into the living room to set up the desk and computer station she was making out of folding tables purchased from Wal-Mart.

Her land phone started ringing. Before she could reach it, her cell phone began to play Bach's Prelude and Fugue in D major. She answered both of them. The land phone was Olivia's secretary, Callie. The other was Olivia.

"I have a job for you," Olivia said. "I interviewed a physician here who just got back from Iraq. He's a pioneer of the new regional pain management they're using for battlefield wounds. He's setting up a training program at Nellis. It's open to anyone affiliated with the troops, wives and so forth. It's work they've been developing at Walter

Reed. It's a spinal block that can be used quickly for even the worst wounds. They're training teams of field medics in the techniques. I told him about you, and that you were getting ready to apply to medical schools. This would look great on a résumé, Winifred. Besides, I can't think of anyone who would be better at it."

"But I don't have an MD. All I have is a degree in science."

"They're training teams, Winifred. There are all sorts of jobs. You can't go to medical school for at least a year, and you need something to do. You'd have the chance to work with cutting-edge technology. I talked to the guy about you. He thought you sounded like what they need."

"I guess I could do it. I was making up beds."

"What?"

"I was making up beds."

"Well, now you're going down to the base medical center and putting in an application for this training. Callie's going to fax you the information. You might have a chance to go over there if you really got in on this. Could you do that?"

"I'll do whatever I have to do."

"Good girl. Look, I have to go. I've got a kid from the university sending me copy from Lebanon. He fell in love with a Lebanese girl and went over there to visit her family. He's been there while the Syrian troops have been leaving. We're printing his pieces every week. Get on this job. We're in a war, Winifred. It's hard to remember that sometimes, but it's true."

"I will. Thanks. Listen, are you coming here to see Bobby?"

"Maybe next week for a few days. I'm going to do a piece for the paper as soon as I get the interviews set up."

"Are you really pregnant, Olivia? You don't sound like you are."

"It's just like normal except you can eat all the time and wear loose clothes. I like it. Look, I have to go."

Olivia hung up, and Winifred finished arranging things in the living room, put the painting notes somewhere where she would never see them again, and went to work reading the faxes that were coming from Olivia's secretary.

At three that afternoon she was at the Nellis Air Force Base hospital, waiting to be interviewed. She had a portfolio of her grades and MCAT scores. She had recommendations from her old professors at Duke, and she had every piece of paper she could imagine them wanting to see. She was wearing flat shoes, a seersucker skirt, and a beautiful white cotton designer blouse that no one would ever guess cost two hundred dollars. I might as well wear one nice thing, she decided. It doesn't hurt to look nice if you want to be taken seriously.

Two hours later she was signed up for a fellowship to study with a group of hand-picked medics from around the United States. There were six medical school graduates doing their internship in the program. A new wing was being added to the existing hospital to house the program, and everyone Winifred talked to was excited and in a hurry. "The hours may be more than you want," one of the directors told her. "Be prepared for that."

"I'm good," she answered. "I can take long hours."

7
DATA, APRIL 2005

Regional pain management. Notes, 2003. 1st Battlefield. Lower leg blown away. Regular pain, ten out of ten. Catheter in lower leg, muscles gone, tibia fractured but holding. Applied tourniquet. Brought to field hospital. Had already received 15 to 18 milligrams of morphine. Still in great pain. Placed a lumbar catheter in a spinal block. Tibia snapped. After fifteen minutes, surgery completed to shore up area; patient was awake, alert, pain free. Culmination of many years of work. Later, used eternal fixator, bone put together, leg saved for sixteen months, then had to be amputated. Prosthetic device working well. Despite valiant efforts to keep the leg, Officer Walker agreed to amputation as venous system beyond repair.

The rehabilitation center at Nellis Air Force Base was not as large as the one at Walter Reed, but it was so high tech that it looked more like a space station than part of a hospital. Lieutenant Brian Kane walked in the automatically opened doors and was met by a six-foot-seven-inch-tall nurse's aide, who saluted him and handed him a form that was already almost completely filled in. "Sorry about this, sir. We try to keep paperwork at a minimum, sir. I got most of it off the computer. I'm Aaron Lightfoot, sir. Civilian, sir. I'm only seventeen."

"You aren't in school?" Brian asked, laughing. The serious, gangly teenager was the last thing he had expected when he left the apartment that morning, annoyed that he had to waste two hours in physical therapy when he didn't want any more advice, exercises, cortisone patches, or reminders that his face had been blown up.

"Why in the hell are they making me do this?" he had asked Winifred.

"To piss you off," she said. "Obviously that could be the only reason."

"I've got work to do."

"Just go to the appointment. I want your face to go back to normal. I don't like that little place where the hair doesn't grow."

She pushed him out the door, then pulled him back and kissed him on the scar tissue. "See, you don't even have feeling there. Damaged goods, that's what I married."

"See if you can get that electrician over here today, okay? I need those outlets in the guest room. We've got to find a bigger place."

"This place is fine. Go on. Get out of here."

Now Brian was leaning on the check-in counter, filling out the forms while the lanky black-haired volunteer watched worshipfully.

"My dad was killed the first week in Afghanistan," Aaron said. "Except for basketball season, I do an internship here in the mornings. I make, well, very good grades. I sort of have a photographic memory, so I don't have to go to school too much. I'm going to start premed classes at the University of Nevada this summer, sir. So, anyway, I'm your man when you're here. I'll check you in, make sure your therapists are waiting, and be available if you need to call."

"Lead on," Brian said. "Let's get on with it."

Twenty minutes later he was reclined in a

comfortable leather chair and a therapist was applying small pads to the injured area. "If you can stand a little stinging, it only takes fourteen minutes," the therapist said. "If it bothers you, we'll turn it down." The therapist was an auburn-haired girl who didn't look much older than Aaron. "I'm Jessica. Aaron will be here unless you'd like him outside the door. There's a television screen. You can watch videos or a film about this process, if you like." She moved a small screen near the chair and nodded to Aaron. He stood at attention beside the screen.

The room in which they were sitting was painted pale gray, with white woodwork. The floor was soft blue tile. The tables and chairs matched the therapy chair. The whole place looked as sterile as an operating room. "Keep your face as still as possible," Aaron said. "Talk if you need to, but it's better if you don't."

"Tell me about your last basketball season," Brian said. "Start with the first game and tell me who you played and if you won."

Aaron turned on the electrodes that activated the cortisone-soaked pads, squinted to make sure everything was where he wanted it, and then began to tell Brian about the Fortier Warriors' past season, which had culminated in a regional final they lost by two points in overtime.

"A lot of guys cried," he added. "My uncle cried. He was home on leave. I don't get it when men cry over basketball games. I never did do that, even when I was a little kid."

War, Brian was thinking. This glorious goddamn kid with no father to watch this flowering. I'm going to cry, goddamnit. Think about something else. Think about wildlife. Think about duck hunting.

"Are you okay?" Aaron asked, squinting. "You want me to turn this down, sir?"

Brian gritted his half-titanium, half-plastic jaw and shook his head. "Okay," he mumbled. "It's okay."

"Don't make any plans for me for Saturday morning," Brian told Winifred that night. "I'm going to watch basketball tryouts at a local high school."

"What's that about?"

"My intern at the rehab center is trying out for starting post for his senior year. He's got competition from a kid who transferred here from New York."

"Okay," Winifred said. "Well, sure. That's good." She looked across the table at this man she had married, and knew that she had not begun to sound the mystery of his being, the breadth of his interests, the boundless life that had been unleashed by the pain and injury he had endured. I'm so lucky, she thought. How did I get lucky enough to marry this man? I'm not that good looking. I'm not interesting like Olivia or Louise. I'm not even all that smart. I'm just hardworking, and at least I stopped being chubby. If I hadn't lost weight for the wedding, Brian would never have looked at me.

"What's that look?" he asked. "What's the sad face?"

"I don't know why you married me," she answered. "I'm still trying to figure it out."

"I wanted a cook and a slave," he said. "I've told you that. Did the electrician come?"

"He put two extra outlets in the guest room."

"Good girl."

Friday night, Tulsa, Oklahoma. Olivia sat in her office, staring at the front-page makeup for Saturday's paper. After a few minutes she got up from the desk and walked across the newsroom and pulled up a chair next to the headline desk.

"I want to lead with the Greyhound bus wreck and the president's visit to Arkansas next week. Put the bombings on the lower left hand. We can't lead with the bombings every day. People recoil and are brutalized. Either they quit caring or they don't let it register. I talked to a psychiatrist in North Carolina about it for an hour last night. She said the overkill takes away the validity."

"Why are you telling me this?"

"Just rearrange it." The skinny headline writer bent over his keyboard and moved things around so that the main headline read, BUSH VISITS PLANT IN ARKANSAS.

"President Bush," Olivia said.

"I'll try. Okay, PRESIDENT BUSH TO VISIT AREA. Is that all right?"

"Then get the bus wreck in the right-hand column."

"It's still death, Olivia."

"All right. What else do we have?"

"The ivory-billed woodpecker thing. That's still alive."

"Get it up there. I'll call someone at the university and get some quotes. Go on, do it."

The skinny writer bent his scrawny shoulders over the computer and reworked the page. In the lower left-hand corner in small letters the headline read, IN IRAQ, BOMBS KILL 40 AND INJURE 100.

Olivia looked around the messy room, with its desks piled with papers and un-capped pens and leftover coffee cartons. She started rubbing her chin with her left hand, an old habit from when she was in grade school. When she had the front page of Saturday's paper the way she wanted it, she thanked the skinny headline writer, told him to go on home, and went back to her office. Then she called a biologist at the University of Tulsa and talked to her for thirty minutes about the sighting of an ivory-billed wood-pecker in central Arkansas. "I had one around my house for three years recently and no one would believe me when I spot-ted it," the biologist said. "I'm an activist in feminist causes, as you know, and people are always gunning for me. Anyway, I didn't believe it myself the first two years. I called the wildlife people and they came out and set up a trap, but I took it down as soon as they left. I stalked it every chance I got. It would start pecking on the house when I took naps in the afternoons. It was May. All three times it was May. My girlfriend was there at least twice and she saw it too. You can call her if you like. Crissie Jennings. She teaches in the political science depart-ment. Her number's —"

"That's okay," Olivia said. "I believe you.

So what happened the third year?"

"It pecked on the house for about a month. I saw it twice more. The goddamn thing was huge. The biggest woodpecker I've ever seen, but I never got a picture of it. I drew it a few times. You want to see the sketches?"

"Yes, can you fax them to me? Would you mind if I put one in the paper?"

"Sure. As soon as we hang up. How many do you want to see?"

"All the ones you have."

An hour later a drawing of a believed-to-be-extinct woodpecker was on the front page of the *Tulsa World*'s Saturday morning edition, replacing a photograph of a blown-up tank. Two hours later, Olivia was at the Tulsa Airport, catching a night flight to Dallas en route to Nevada. By the time the twenty-passenger Air Tulsa flight took off, a storm was moving in from the gulf coast, carrying hail and tornadoes. Olivia didn't give a damn if the storm blew the airplane to California. "I'm going to see my husband," she told the Wal-Mart executive who was the only other person on the flight. "Where are you heading?"

"I'm going home," he said. "My little girl is going to her prom tomorrow night. I have to be there to dance with her."

"Olivia Tree," Olivia said, extending her hand. "I bought some junk food in the airport. If you get hungry, tell me."

"I've got a couple of train bottles of scotch," he answered. "We'll share."

8
BLESSINGS

April 29, 2005, Nellis Air Force Base, Nevada. Bobby picked Olivia up from the airport at nine at night and took her to a resort near the air base that catered to servicemen and their visitors. It was a beautiful resort run by the Four Seasons Hotels. Bobby had heard about it from Winifred the week before.

"I love this place," Olivia said. "Don't ever tell me how much it costs." She was settled into a large room overlooking a golf course, and below was a swimming pool with a waterfall, surrounded by beautiful pale blue beach umbrellas. She had tried out all the sofas and chairs and then climbed up on the king-size bed. "It's just like Winifred to come to an air force base and find a resort nearby."

"I really like her," Bobby said. "And her husband, Brian. He's been in and out of my unit a lot the past few weeks. I never saw anybody pay less attention to themselves. He has to wear these patches on the side of his face, and he just pulls them off when he wants to talk to you and sticks them on his uniform, and then he sticks them back on. They have cortisone in them to make the stitches heal. He told me he'd go back to Iraq in a minute if he could get sent. He wants so much to fly the drones, but his vision got messed up enough that he can't. You have to have perfect hand-eye coordination to fly them. But he knows how to check them to make them work. That's what he's doing here. Fine-tuning. I'm not supposed to talk about anything we do, and I'm *not* talking about it. I just can't get over how they work. I'm taking this course twice a week on electricity and sound waves and a bunch of really interesting science. I would have paid attention in school if they'd had teachers like the one I have here. There's this guy from MIT who's the worst genius you ever saw in your life. I really want you to meet him someday. He can make you think you understand things that are so complex you'd give up if you read them in a book."

"I'm jealous," Olivia said. "I want to be here with you and be doing what you are doing. I want to quit my goddamn job and come out here and help with this. No one in the United States has any idea of what is going on in the military or who we are up against. They forget it more than they remember. I get depressed trying to think up ways to explain what I know. I can't print half the stuff I know or I'd lose readers. I can't talk about science or mechanics or drone airplanes in any depth, and it frustrates me."

"I'm missing you, is what I'm mostly doing," Bobby said. He moved nearer and began to touch her breasts and stomach with his hand. "I miss all this. I'm horny and I'm lonely and I want to tell you things. It's not all good, Olivia. I can't tell you about the strikes, but I don't like doing it to populated places. Still, I know we have to go there. They hide in houses with women and children. They treat women like shit over there. Brian told me stuff I don't even want to know."

"What are you doing to my stomach?" Olivia moved closer. She was starting to get turned on, and she didn't care anymore about drone airplanes or war or anything else. She didn't care about anything except getting off the rest of her clothes and the rest of his and maybe remembering to have

9
CHOICES

May 2, 2005, Tulsa, Oklahoma. Olivia woke at 5 a.m., pulled herself out of bed, and went to the window to watch a thunderstorm pound against the maple trees outside her window. In a neighbor's yard an apple tree that had burst into bloom a few days before was being bent almost to the ground by the wind. Tornado watch, Olivia decided, and turned on the television long enough to hear the news. More violence on the Palestinian-Israeli borders. A runaway bride in Duluth, Georgia, was about to be charged with filing a false kidnapping report and might be fined a hundred thousand dollars to pay for the police overtime during the three-day search. The film *The Hitchhiker's Guide to the Galaxy* had made $21.7 million its first weekend at the box office, and the young woman who had been filmed holding a prisoner on a leash at Abu Ghraib prison in Baghdad was awaiting sentencing in

North Carolina.

Olivia had come in from her trip to Nevada at eleven o'clock the night before and had gone to bed without brushing her teeth or washing her face. She had slept restlessly all night, waking to the rain and thunder, thirsty, her nose stopped up from allergies.

I can't do this, she decided. Six months ago I was a powerful, in-shape, productive woman thrilled to get up every morning and worry about circulation and advertising profits and how to run the show at the *Tulsa World,* and now I am a sniveling, sick, allergic hypochondriac who is doing a really crappy job of carrying a child in my womb. I'm going to see Kathleen this morning and get a complete checkup and find a way to deal with these allergies. At least they'll be better today, because it's raining.

As she watched the TV, tornado warnings were beginning to appear on the crawl at the bottom of the screen.

Olivia went into the bathroom and took a shower, then put on a seersucker robe and pushed a button on a remote control to brew coffee in the kitchen. Next she went into her workroom and started pounding out an editorial for Tuesday's paper.

When she had written four sentences, she went to a laptop and set the screen to follow the sentencing of the Abu Ghraib guard, a five-foot-tall, twenty-two-year-old girl from a farm in West Virginia who was about to be sent to prison for doing what she thought the military wanted her to do. "This is it," the editorial began.

I can no longer be quiet about the insanity of blaming twenty-two-year-old soldiers for overreacting when we take them from small, unsophisticated lives, barely train them, send them off to a fiercely hot, sandblasted terror of a country that they didn't even know existed and about which their half-assed educations in public schools taught them nothing, tell them the enemy is the devil and that it is up to them to protect the *entire United States of America* plus all their family and friends from nuclear, biological, and chemical warfare (imminent, planned attacks that we may or may not be able to thwart in time), and set them to work guarding large numbers of highly trained, deadly, furious, and frightened prisoners, and then expect them, without any psychological training or oversight, to treat these same scary prisoners with professional and dignified strategies.

These kids were scared to death. What do you do when you are scared? You strike out. It's a wonder the abuses were not more widespread and worse. Every scared citizen of the United States secretly hoped and believed that the government of the United States and the United States military and intelligence forces were questioning prisoners with every means possible to find out what was going to happen next and where and how the terrorists were going to strike next. *Anyone* with *any sense* knows *what* these soldiers thought they were supposed to do, whether they were given orders or not given orders to solicit information from prisoners by whatever means available.

Where is common sense? Where is comprehension? Where in the name of heaven is the justification for treating these young, scared, unprepared soldiers as though they had thought up *for themselves* some unimaginable behaviors and carried out those behaviors? I have talked to thirty-year-old men who were in Iraq who say they are still shaking sand out of their hair and ears and minds months after they returned from combat. Not to mention the nightmares and the damaged body parts and the abiding fear that they will have to return to the godforsaken place.

The rest of the media can continue to play their coy, enabling game of tiptoeing around the truths of this conflict, but I was raised to tell the truth, and I get sick when I play around with it.

We went to Iraq to make a statement about what happens if you defy and attack the United States of America, to protect our ally Israel, to protect the oil fields in the area, to make certain that Saddam Hussein did not have nuclear weapons, and to destroy all weapons of any kind that he did have before he used them to supply al-Qaeda, and because the American public, I myself included, wanted revenge.

I am married to a marine who is on active duty. I am five months pregnant with our child. I have skin in this game. I want some cards on the table.

Olivia checked her e-mails, went into her bedroom, pulled on a dress and some panty hose and a pair of medium-heeled shoes, combed her hair back into a ponytail, and left the house carrying a hard copy of the piece she had just written. She didn't want to trust it to the computer.

At ten minutes to eight she reached the newspaper building parking lot, parked in her reserved space, and went into the building, still seething.

Callie Mayfield was already at her desk. "Get me some breakfast from McDonald's," Olivia said. "And a large coffee, please. How you doing? You doing okay?"

"I'm okay. There's a funnel cloud near Healing Springs."

"It's okay. I really need something to eat."

"I'm going." Callie got up from her desk, took a raincoat from a rack, and started away. "Eggs, bacon, toast, all right?"

"Perfect. There's money in the jar on my desk."

"I know."

"Stop worrying about me, Callie. Just get me some food."

"All right."

Olivia sat down at her desk, edited the editorial slightly, read it again, and got up and walked across the newsroom and handed it to the editorial page editor. "Don't mess with it," she told him. "Just like it is."

"All right," he answered. He never argued with Olivia, just as he had never argued with the last editor or the one before that. He had two married daughters and grandchildren getting ready for college. He liked his job and he intended to keep it.

Callie returned with Olivia's breakfast, and Olivia ate it slowly and carefully and then went into the bathroom to brush her teeth. She started bleeding as soon as she got up and started walking. Not profusely, but enough so that she had blood running down her legs by the time she reached a sink. She mopped it up with paper towels and turned to a secretary coming out of a stall. "Get Callie Mayfield," she told her. "Get her now."

"What's wrong?"

"I'm bleeding. Get her in here. I may need you too."

Half an hour later they had made their way from downtown Tulsa in a torrential downpour and were turning into the parking lot of a new doctor's building. A nurse came out the side door and helped Olivia into an examining room. In a few minutes, Olivia's old friend Kathleen Whitman was beside her, and the nurse followed with a hypodermic needle and gave her a shot. Two other nurses undressed her and set up a drip beside the table.

"We'll put you in the hospital for a few days," Kathleen said. "Don't panic, Olivia. These things happen. They don't always end in miscarriages. Half the time, all you need is bed rest."

"Oh, God."

"Have you been under stress?"

"What do you think?" Olivia said with a laugh. It was the first light moment. "Goddamn, I love you, Kat. Do with me what you will. You're the doctor; I'm the patient."

"Hold that thought. We're going to add a light sedative to the drip, Olivia. I know you want to be calm, and I just want to be sure you are."

"Anything you want. Save my son, Kathleen. I want this baby. This one right here, not another one."

"I'll try." Kathleen put her hand on Olivia's arm as the sedative began to take effect. Olivia and Kathleen had run hundreds of miles together on the University of Tulsa outdoor track and on the trails in the park and around the hospital's quarter-mile track when Kathleen first started practicing medicine. They didn't see much of each other now that both of them had busy careers, but the bonds they had formed in their running days were strong.

"I'd have let you be my doctor when you were fifteen years old," Olivia mumbled. "You go ahead. Do what you want to do. Call Bobby, Callie, but don't scare him. No, don't call him — scratch that."

Olivia slept.

She was still somewhat sedated when the reaction to her inflammatory editorial began the following day. "What were you thinking?" Big Jim Walters asked as gently as he could. He was standing by her hospital bed holding a bunch of flowers his secretary had bought for him to take to Olivia.

"I wasn't thinking," she answered. "I was reacting."

"Well, now they are reacting. Much of it is positive. I'll say that. But you've brought the university nuts out in full force."

"Fuck them."

"Okay. Well, how are you doing in here? Is this going to go on much longer, do you think?"

"I don't know, Jim. I may have to take a leave of absence. My cousin's an internist, and she called and said for me to settle down and get ready for some serious bed rest. Oh, God, there's my doctor. You know Kathleen, don't you? Who used to be my running buddy? Now she's an obstetrician, for God's sake. Kat, come in. You know Jim."

"I'll wait outside," Jim said. "I'll just wait out there."

Kathleen screwed up her mouth and tried to look serious and professional, which is possible with close personal friends, but sometimes tricky.

"You have to stay in bed, maybe for weeks, maybe a few months. I think we can stop this, but you can't walk around."

"I knew this would happen. My cousin Susan already called and told me."

"Can your aunt Mary Lily stay with you?"

"I suppose so. Call Jim back in here, would you? I'll tell him."

"I have to stay in bed for a while, and I'm burned out anyway," Olivia told him when he came back into the room, still holding the flowers. "Put the flowers down."

"For how long?"

"Six months. I need to have this baby, and I need to stay home and take care of it. I'm tired of the rat race, Jim. I don't like the work anymore. I might not come back at all."

"Don't say that."

"I never intended to be a goddamn editor.

I'm a writer. I wanted to write books."

"Olivia."

"What?"

"Let's don't burn bridges."

"I'm on a bunch of drugs right now. Maybe we should talk next week. You want me to write a follow-up to the editorial?"

"No, I'll have Cameron do it. Wait until they sentence her, then write it. I'm not mad about the piece, Olivia, I liked it."

"Yeah, you're mad. You should be. Are they canceling subscriptions?"

"Some are."

"Okay. Thanks for the flowers, old friend."

He stood at the foot of the bed looking down at the five-foot-four-inch dynamo he had brought in to save his empire. He still believed she could do it if she would. It's true about women, he decided. They don't give a damn about making money; they just like to spend it.

Olivia didn't want to talk to him anymore. She wanted to go back to sleep and think about how glad she was that her baby was all right. Her little boy, the one she was going to watch play ball and teach to ride and take with Little Sun to sit before the earth island and listen to the earth and sky and trees and plants, and take to the zoo to see the elephants and zebras and chimpanzees.

She fell asleep thinking of her father in North Carolina and how serious he had been at her wedding. She thought about him going outside to find his overseer, Lucas, and telling Lucas about Olivia's being pregnant, and the way they'd talk about it. She started laughing deep down inside herself in a place that was not touched by the chaos of the outside world or war or the death of innocents or madness or politicians or the glaciers melting in Alaska or in the Antarctic, or by the fate of that poor, scared kid, Pfc. Lynndie England, who had held an Iraqi prisoner on a leash in a dungeon in a country she had never heard of until she got sent there to survive or die, because she was too poor to get an education any other way except to join the United States Army Reserve. Who the fuck do we think we are to blame our sins on this poor girl? Olivia was thinking. What in the fuck do we think we are doing?

It fell to Louise to tell the family that Olivia had taken a leave of absence from her job. "Oh, no, oh, my God," Jessie said.

"She's been unhappy with the job for a while," Tallulah said.

"She never likes to do anything for a long time," Winifred declared.

"No one in this family finishes what they start," Winifred's brother Lynley proclaimed.

"Well, to hell with it," Olivia's father said. "Good for her. You can't serve two masters. I'm starting to think working isn't all I used to think it was anyway."

10

THE DAZZLING RETURN OF THE REAL EARTH IN SPRING WHEN NEW LEAVES ARE ENOUGH TO DRIVE A MAN TO WONDER AND SMALL BIRDS ARE LEARNING TO FLY

In the Mississippi Sound, pods of dolphins
Hoist up their cubs to the oxygen-laden air
Yesterday I walked past a Catholic school
Where a circle of eight-year-old children,
Holding flowers, were saying the rosary,
Hail Mary, full of grace, blessed art thou
    among women
And blessed is the fruit of thy womb,
    blessed, blessed,
Blessed, blessed . . .

The goddamn beautiful world, Olivia woke
up thinking. She started to get out of bed,
then remembered and called to her aunt

instead. "I know you're awake, Mary Lily. Please come here and open the windows and let the spring come in."

"I got your breakfast ready if you want it," Mary Lily answered. "And your dad called at six this morning and said he was coming. He said he was bringing you a wheelchair his daddy used that was real easy to get around in."

"He's driving?"

"I guess he is. He said he'd be here late tonight and was it okay if he got here late, and I said we'd have food waiting for him."

Mary Lily bent over the bed and kissed Olivia on the forehead, then opened the long windows that went out onto an unused balcony. "I'm going to get Philip up here to screen these windows and put in some of those doors that open out. We can put you a little daybed out there."

"This isn't going to last that long, Aunt Lily. I'll be up before he could get it finished."

"Well, he's coming today to see about it." Mary Lily left the room and returned with a breakfast tray that held coffee and toast and boiled eggs. It had been two weeks since Olivia was snatched out of the real world and put to bed and ordered to stay completely still, except when she went to the bathroom. She had started bleeding in the fifth month of her pregnancy, and her good friend and obstetrician, Kathleen, was not taking any chances.

"How will you know when I can get up?" Olivia had asked her the day before.

"When you haven't had any symptoms."

"I haven't had any since you put me to bed."

"Good. I want to keep it that way. Are you worried about your job?"

"I'm taking a leave of absence. Good thing too. Some people are really mad about the Lynndie England editorial."

"Do you care?"

"Hell, no. I'm sleeping better since I wrote it. It's one of about sixty issues that were driving me crazy, having to pussyfoot around. I want Jim to let me write a column. I could get it syndicated. I know I could."

"He won't?"

"He hasn't called me back about it."

Outside Olivia's bedroom windows the baby mockingbirds were getting better at flying every day. It was the main happiness she had every morning. She watched them now while Mary Lily sat beside her on the bed, feeding her. On the tray with her food was a small fork and knife she had used when she was a child. Mary Lily had bought it at a yard sale in Healing Springs when Olivia was four years old. It was a "youth set" of plated silver with aquamarine stones in the handles. How Mary Lily had found it in her kitchen, Olivia could not imagine; nor did she question it. She was so accustomed to being adored by her aunt, who was just fifteen years older, that she just accepted it as her due.

"So what's going on with you and Philip Whitehorse?" Olivia asked. "Are you talking or are you holding your cards to your chest? You might as well go on and tell me about it. You know I'll get it out of you."

"He's coming over about ten this morning. He has to help Kayo feed horses; then he's coming over in his truck to see about putting in some of those screened doors that open out. He might paint the porch. If you had that fixed, it would give you a place to sit and write your book."

"I couldn't write a book if I was outside. I'd just be watching the birds and sky and wishing I could get to the country. If we were home, we could go walking down into the woods to watch the winter ponds start drying out. A man up in New England wrote a poem about how trees take the winter ponds and turn them into summer leaves. I'll show it to you. And I meant, are you going to admit you got a thing for Philip?"

"I haven't got a thing."

"Yes, you do. Go on and go to bed with him, Mary Lily. You've got the whole house. No one will know if it happens in Tulsa. Then you can see if you want to marry him. It would be all right if you left Grandmother and Granddaddy. You don't have to live your life taking care of people."

"He's already got a wife. She's a drunkard. She lives down in Oklahoma City and she gets mad when their daughter goes to see him. Their daughter is as fat as Miss Drago. I don't know what I'd want to get into that mess for."

"Because he's a good man and you've known him all your life, and you don't have to ever see his drunkard wife and fat daughter. All you have to do is admit you get excited every time he's coming over. I want you to put on some clothes that fit before he gets here. Put on those black jeans and a pretty shirt and bring a brush in here and let me work on your hair."

Mary Lily stood up. She was five feet eleven inches tall, and when she stood up straight and held herself proudly, she was as handsome as her father, Little Sun, and as

224

imposing. Mostly she kept that all under the table, as if it were bad taste to be taller and more powerful than other people.

Olivia moved the breakfast tray and very carefully stood up and walked into the bathroom. It had been two weeks since there had been blood, but every time she stood up, she feared it might start again. She had sunk into the routine of staying in bed and no longer resented it, but the fear stayed with her. Stay in there, baby boy, she whispered to herself. You're safe with me. I would never let anything happen to you.

She had watched a Discovery Channel program about a group of elephants and how the whole group cared for the beautiful babies. She had added an old concern to the list of things she was going to write about when she got her column: the capturing and putting into cages of elephants, dolphins, and maybe any other mammal. Except you can't stop at that; you have to include research on animals, and I'm not ready to go that far yet.

Daniel Hand had flown to New Orleans to see Olivia's sister, Jessie, and her husband and their children. He had rented a Lincoln Navigator at a luxury car rental place and was getting ready to leave for Oklahoma.

225

He had meant to set out earlier, but Jessie had insisted he have breakfast with the children before he started driving. "I want to send my maternity clothes to Olivia," she said. "And I have to go up in the attic to find the box."

Now the back of the Navigator was packed with long, square boxes holding the elaborate wardrobe of maternity clothes Jessie's mother-in-law, Crystal Manning, had bought for her. "Okay," Jessie said, "I want you to take a photograph of her, Daddy. I want to see Olivia pregnant. I'll never believe it until I see it."

"Come with me. Take the kids out of school for a few days. It wouldn't hurt them."

"I can't. King has ball games. If he didn't go, he might not be on first base. He wants to be on first base."

"I want to pitch," his ten-year-old grandson said. "But she won't let me."

"Why not?" Daniel asked. "Why can't he pitch?"

"Because he'll ruin his shoulder. . . ."

Daniel got up and went around the table and patted his grandson on the shoulders and started making his escape.

"She won't let him pitch," he told his

overseer on the phone as soon as he was out of Uptown New Orleans and on the highway leading west to Oklahoma. "She won't let him pitch on his baseball team. I swear to God, Lucas. My daddy was right about women. You let them take over and they'll ruin the children. Now I got to go up to Oklahoma, where the daughter I thought was going to get something done in the world is flat on her back in bed, about to die in childbirth like her mother did."

"Calm down, boss. They don't die anymore. They're too mean to die of anything. I heard she quit her job running the newspaper. Niall told me the other day. He came by to get some papers out of your desk."

"To sell the cottage on the island. It's falling down and nobody wants to go there."

"It was good fishing. Those oysters were the best I ever had. I hate for you to sell that, boss."

"I'm in a bunch of trucks. I got to pay attention. Ten four."

Daniel put both hands on the wheel and started really driving. Two grandsons and another one on the way. He was getting out of this woman life he'd been leading since he was twenty and started getting women pregnant. He drove in peace, planning summers on his farm when the grandsons would come to visit without their mothers, and they could live like men and pitch baseballs ten hours a day if they wanted to.

Eight hours later he crossed the state line into Oklahoma. At five that afternoon he was in Tulsa, squinting over the monitor of the five-star navigation system he had paid an extra six dollars a day to have in the automobile. He eased off Yale Avenue and onto Third Street and down to a streetlight and then straight to Olivia's house. He parked in the driveway and went up the flower-covered path to the doorway and rang the bell, and Mary Lily ran to the door and let him in.

In another two minutes he was standing at the foot of Olivia's bed. She had been watching a financial news program called *Mad Money* and making notes on a legal pad for stocks she could buy for the baby's trust fund, when she got enough money to make him a trust fund.

"Oh, Daddy," she said, pushing a remote to turn off the television. "I'm glad you're here. It's so boring lying here. But it's what I have to do. What's happening? How's Jessie?"

He bent his tall body and kissed her on the side of the face. Mary Lily was behind him pulling up a chair, and he sat down in it and surveyed the scene. Olivia's bed was piled high with books and magazines and notepads. Her laptop sat precariously on a hospital table above the bed. Beside the laptop was a tray holding bowls and cups and a prayer flag that Crow had woven for her and sent with Mary Lily.

"I quit my job," Olivia went on. "I'm going to write a book. Well, I might write a column for them, if I can get what I want in a contract."

"We're mighty happy about the boy, the baby," Daniel began. "Jessie's boys are good boys; they're getting big enough to take out places. She sent you a bunch of clothes. You want me to go get them out of the car?"

"Not yet." Olivia laughed and pushed papers and books out of her way. "Stack some of this stuff on the floor, would you, Dad? Never mind. Look, go down to the living room and I'll join you. I can go downstairs twice a day if I don't walk. I'll be down there in a minute."

"I could carry you," Daniel said. "I used to carry Mother when she got old."

"It's not that bad." Olivia laughed again. "I'm going in next week for tests. We might be out of this bed in a few days."

Daniel got up, backed out of the room,

and followed Mary Lily down the stairs to the sparsely furnished, very contemporary living room, which Olivia had copied out of a magazine called *Real Simple*. It had light-colored board floors, window shades from Pier 1, and wide, comfortable chairs with colored cushions. In a corner beside French doors was a long red leather chaise with a blue leather chair beside it. "Sit in the blue chair," Mary Lily directed. "I'm going to get you something to drink. We have home-made stew and potatoes and fresh peas for dinner. I hope you're going to be hungry."

"I already am. How're your parents, Mary Lily? They doing all right?"

"They're glad you can come. It's hard keeping her in bed. She never stops moving."

"But the baby, the boy's all right?"

"She just got tired."

Olivia got out of bed and put on a clean white and blue seersucker robe and slippers. Then she washed her face and combed her hair and went to the stairs, where she sat on the top step and went down them slowly, without standing up. At the bottom of the stairs she finally stood, pulled back her shoulders, and walked into the living room to join her father.

"What kind of book are you writing?" he asked her.

"Not like Aunt Anna's, Daddy. I'm a journalist. I'll write about the war. I don't know what yet. Maybe vignettes from a newspaper editor's point of view. Interviews with people whose lives are involved. When I get out to Nevada I'll write about that. How we are using technology to stay on top, if we can stay on top, if we can train enough people to run the machines we make, our education system from the ground up, how fucking — excuse me — spoiled this country is and how we can get less spoiled before it's too late. We will. I have faith in the United States. If you could stay long enough, we could go out to Nevada together and you could see what Bobby's doing. He flies an airplane, sometimes helicopters, in Iraq, from a console in a building in Nevada. He's a copilot now, but some of the smaller planes he flies alone. He's good at it, Daddy. He told me the other day it wasn't that much different from riding horses, rodeoing."

"I'd like to see it."

"We've got you a room fixed up."

"I'll just stay at a hotel, if you don't mind, sweet sister. I don't want to be on top of you here. I like your little house, though;

it's a friendly-looking place."

While Olivia and Daniel were talking, Mary Lily set Daniel a place at the dining room table and brought in a bowl of stew, along with a second bowl of small red potatoes and fresh peas and carrots. To that she added homemade bread and butter and iced tea and a slice of caramel cake.

"Come get your supper," she said, coming back into the living room. "I've got enough trouble getting Olivia to eat anything. I could use a person with a normal appetite."

Daniel stood up and followed Mary Lily into the dining room, and Olivia joined them at the table.

"This looks mighty good," Daniel said. "I've had this stew before when your momma made it for me in Tahlequah. What's in this? I got a man at my house who can cook anything if he has the recipe."

"It has beef and venison, and sometimes chicken or pork, and tomatoes and carrots and okra, if we can get it, and corn, which is why Momma only likes to make it when there is corn in the garden. It's the fresh vegetables that make it so good. Momma doesn't know a thing about organic gardening. She just never puts poison on anything. If she wants to keep worms off the tomatoes and corn, she puts bowls of beer under the plants. You think the Cherokees are bad to drink alcohol, you should see how many worms climb in those bowls to die." Mary Lily started laughing, something she didn't do that often in public. She mostly liked to laugh by herself or, lately, with Philip Whitehorse when they were alone.

"Stay here tonight, Daddy," Olivia said. "We want a man in the house. You can go to a hotel tomorrow if you like, but I want you to be here in the morning."

"Then I will," Daniel agreed. "Now tell me everything you know about the work Bobby is doing. I'm interested in this. He just sits at a console? Is he alone with a copilot in a cubicle?"

"No, it's a long, curved console like air traffic controllers use. I asked him that myself. He said it's so simple, really. You have a screen and information from the people on the ground in Iraq and you just steer the plane and shoot and release rockets, and it's just exactly like a video game, and the very best person doing it with him is a man from Tulsa who misspent his youth playing video games. . . ."

An hour later, Daniel was propped up on pillows in the guest bedroom, reading the information Olivia had pulled up on the computer from Boeing and Northrop Grumman and all the companies that were building the planes and helicopters and guidance systems of the drone aircraft. Before he went to sleep, Daniel had put in a call to his stockbroker in Charlotte to sell his Pfizer stock and invest the money in some of the companies who were building the planes. "Call me back early," he said in the message. "And why in the hell didn't Merrill Lynch mention this to me?"

As soon as her father went to bed, Olivia scooted back up the stairs on her derriere and climbed into her bed and was just getting settled when the phone rang. It was Big Jim Walters. "Are you all right?" he asked.

"I'm fine. I'll be done with this bed thing next week, I think. What's up?"

"You need to write a catch-up editorial on the Lynndie England thing. I've got phone numbers for her lawyers. I had it sent to your computer."

"What about the column I was going to write while I'm gone? Why can't it be the first column?"

"All right, if you want to start off with something that's going to piss off half the readers."

"It won't be inflammatory. I've been doing research. She's not very bright, Jim. She was in a mechanics' backup group in the fucking reserves. She's from West Virginia. What in the hell were they doing sending this untrained, not very bright kid to guard Iraqi insurgents in a makeshift prison? When will bigger heads roll? Why did they make this pint-size, pregnant woman the fall guy for the whole Mideast shit storm?"

"That sounds inflammatory."

"Well, I'll tone it down."

"They demoted the general in charge."

"A reserve unit general trained for combat support duty. This has legs for a column, Jim. I'll be careful with it. Just the facts as I can find them."

"All right. Go ahead. When can you do it?"

"Now. I'll send it over in the morning."

"We miss you here."

"No, you don't. The paper looks great. Who's running things?"

"I am. I'm too lazy to look for anyone this week."

Olivia picked up her laptop and began to type. "Don't worry," she told her baby. "You don't need my brain, do you? You've got the womb and access to the blood supply and I ate dinner like a pig, so you should be okay. Go to sleep and grow some bones and shoulders like your daddy's, but don't grow my skin. I want you dark enough to be chief someday. Don't come out looking like some Irish half-breed."

Olivia started playing with first lines for her column: "Why in the name of God did we send a reserve unit of people trained to be *mechanics* into the heart of Iraq to be *prison guards,* outnumbered two hundred to one, under the command of a man whose civilian job had been to run a prison, and expect this reserve unit of mechanics, without adequate training, to have the slightest notion of how to protect their own lives in this dangerous situation, much less extract information from their prisoners, all of this in a prison where Saddam Hussein had killed and brutally tortured and raped thousands of men and women for years? Imagine the karma, imagine the smells, imagine the scene.

"So the main fall guy is going to be a five-foot-tall, twenty-two-year-old girl from West Virginia, who became pregnant with the baby of her superior officer, the ex–prison commander. She is the one to go to jail for the sins of the world? She is to be the sacrifice? We should thank her for going to Iraq, for continuing to *breathe* and survive while this went on around her.

"Where is she in the meantime? Is she with her six-month-old son? Does she have friends to help her? The army doesn't want to answer these questions, but I'm going to keep on asking them."

Olivia printed the pages, set them on the table beside her bed, and went back to the computer. She began putting together a list of ideas for columns.

How the Baltic nations sang for their freedom at the end of the cold war.

Conversations in New York in the late 1980s with a chauffeur who had been the Latvian minister of materials under the Soviet Union.

Monday: 8 Killed, 150 wounded in Baghdad.

Tuesday: 40 killed, 69 wounded, including a four-year-old child. Where are the suicide bombers coming from? What can we do to stop them?

Will Bobby's drone airplanes be patrolling the Syrian border?

North Koreans ready for nuclear test. North Korea is China's pit bull, contained for how long?

Floods in Idaho. Fires in Minnesota. The

Kentucky Derby, what a bunch of bored rich people, what a crowded, unhappy-looking place. A young woman married to an older man who had a horse in the race cried. She cried with her little face-lifted face pressed into his two-thousand-dollar designer jacket while her teenage stepchildren stood sadly by.

Is anyone raising children to know they are part of the human race and that they have to work to keep the free nations of the world strong and free? I think not. I will raise my sons and daughters to dream of being valuable to their fellow men.

Got to call Tallulah tomorrow and see how she's getting along at Vanderbilt. Got to call Susan and thank her for being a physician when she could have lived on her daddy's money. Got to stay in touch with valuable people doing hard work; got to shore them up and set an example by not quitting my job.

She stopped typing. Oh, shit, she thought. Well, I'll call Jim tomorrow and talk to him. He's standing by. He knows it's the baby calling the shots. You calling the shots down there, little buddy? Well, listen, it won't do any good for me to stay home and wait on you hand and foot if the world you have to live in for the next hundred years is in bad shape. So get ready for day care. It's good; you get to catch colds and practice your social skills.

Olivia had just started writing a clean second draft of the column when the phone rang. "It's Jim," the caller said. "Hang on to your chair. Get this, Olivia, just in on the AP. The woman general in charge of Abu Ghraib is being demoted to colonel. You heard that, I suppose? She was arrested for shoplifting in Florida right before they shipped her to Iraq. I'll have to check it before we can print it, but it's on the AP. I've got a call into Reuters."

"Find out what she stole," Olivia answered. "That's the column. Plus, think how bored they must be on those bases when there is no war or they aren't being sent to a war. Would you join the army or run for office, or would I or any sane person not driven by dire need or an ego so out of whack it can't be controlled? We'd be lost if it weren't for the young men and women from small towns who are brainwashed in churches or by servicemen fathers who came back alive or barely wounded and got pensions they like."

"Keep writing, Olivia. But remember, just the facts, and ones we can prove. Don't try to make points and don't blame or judge. And no, I wouldn't run for office, but I was in the navy during the Vietnam War. I'm surprised you didn't know that. I joined when I was seventeen. It was over before I had to go to a war zone, and I got an education courtesy of the United States government. I'm grateful for it."

"Why did you join the navy?"

"I don't know. I guess I wanted to see the ocean."

11
LOUISE

Carl was never at home. He had been assigned to the Pentagon, where his work was to create recruitment campaigns in the South and lower Midwest. At least three days a week he flew out early in the morning and returned after midnight. He was the leader of a three-man group that went to high schools and colleges and lectured and answered questions about the marines. He was cheerful and intelligent and people liked him. He looked like the athlete he had been; on the flights he even worked out with pulleys and hand weights to keep up the appearance of perfect health. On days when he was at home, he rose at dawn and was at his office by eight.

"I'm a paper soldier," he told Brian when he talked to him on the phone. "I've never been in a war zone. The two men who work with me have been everywhere. One was in the Gulf War; the other man was in the invasion of Afghanistan when he was twenty. I'm just the upper-middle-class pretty boy."

"What's the problem, Bro?" Brian asked. "You want me to shoot off your chin so you won't feel guilty? I get a lot of sympathy for it, I'll admit that. Winifred's my slave if she thinks I'm in pain."

"You still taking pills for it?"

"No. I threw them away. They fuck up my head. You can ignore the pain once you learn how. They taught me these breathing tricks. I wish I'd known them when we were playing ball. Hey, I've got a Little League team. Did I tell you that? Olivia Hand's husband, Bobby Tree, is out here. He's a good man. He's flying the unmanned Fire Scouts and training on the Predators. Anyway, he's helping with the team. We've got a tournament in July. You ought to come out and see some of the games."

"I got to hang up, Bro. They're sending me to Fort Smith, Arkansas. We're cleaning up in Arkansas lately. A kid just out of basic training took his sister to her prom dance in Hot Springs last month. He was wearing his dress uniform. The next week we had ten recruits. Ten, baby, and three of them were young women. When's this tournament your team's in?"

"Seventeenth to the twentieth."

"Maybe we'll come."

Louise was writing her cousin Winifred a letter. She had started to send an e-mail, then decided her message was too personal to trust to a system that was monitored by the Pentagon and the CIA.

Dear Winnie,

Do you know that our children will be almost double first cousins? My momma had three double first cousins. Momma and her sister Ariane (Crystal Weiss's mother) had an older sister named Margaret, and she married the brother of my grandfather James Hand, whose name was Niall, like our uncle, only all of them moved to New England and went to Unitarian colleges and some of them were ministers. Anyway, they never had much to do with any of our family except to write to Momma now and then. Uncle Niall is doing a family tree to give to all of us next Christmas. So they are all in it.

The reason I'm writing you is this: Are we right to be in this war? Did we have to start this war? Can we ever stop being there? What are those people thinking when they are being blown up every day if they leave their homes? What should we do? How can anyone know what to do? I'm reading Tom Friedman. He's the only person who makes sense to me. I've lost all ambition to do my own work. I have no idea what I want to say. I'm reading Rilke. It's soothing to me to read the *Duino Elegies.* I know, you told me once he was dependent on the worst sort of Eurotrash, but what poet wasn't dependent on rich people? We're rich people, or we used to be. That doesn't make us bad. Our ancestors were in the Revolutionary War.

I'm usually in a better mood than this.

Love,
Louise

Dear Louise,

How would I know what to do?

I am married to a war hero. He's been there and he got blown up and he says we have to be there because we had to draw a line in the sand and the only thing that matters is that *the United States has not been attacked on our soil* since we went on the offensive in Afghanistan.

He does say he thinks there should be a draft because it isn't fair for poor people to fight the wars, but it's always been that way and it isn't going to change. There is only one member of Congress who has a child in the war. I may be dumb, but I know pragmatism when I see it.

Brian has to go back in for more surgery. There's an infection around his remaining molars. He lost some teeth on that side, but they had saved others. Now he'll probably lose those too. He says he refuses to fixate on a couple of teeth when doctors can make perfectly good ones out of plastic. He's been on antibiotics for a month. I try not to think about all the drugs he's taken or what it's doing to his liver.

You are married to the prospective donor, so it's your *problema también, no es verdad?*

So now I don't care about the right or wrong of a war against people who beat and torture and mass-murder their fellow citizens, and blow up everything every day and kill children and women, and train children to wear time bombs and believe they'll go to a heaven where they can rape virgins all day, to name a few of the reasons I'm glad Brian is still a marine and I'm a marine's wife.

I feel like I'm leaving the rest of the United States to their stupid television programs. When did the whole country ever fight to save itself except the Second World War, and the media are still trying to blame us for things like putting the Japanese into camps until we ascertained they weren't going to be a fifth column.

I'm searching the dictionary every day for new words to talk about the things I can't stop thinking.

Your flag-waver cousin,
Winifred
P.S. Olivia is in bed for three weeks. She was bleeding. Is that unusual? You should call her or send her a card.

Dear Winnie,

I already knew about Olivia. Tallulah called me and so did Jessie.

I think about the war every day. I've started to be a news addict, although Carl says the news is only about 40 percent accurate and all of it is biased.

He says more people get killed every day in automobile accidents in the United States than get killed in Iraq, but I say the injuries aren't as devastating.

Besides, I still believe the war is mainly about oil. And even though it's also to protect the United States, how do we know we're doing the right thing?

Daddy says we should build nuclear power plants. He says if we built smaller ones and more different kinds and really trained people to run them, it would be better than depending on oil. He is reading some physicist named Freeman Dyson, but the books he likes best are all out of print. He says the big oil companies keep us from having safe nuclear power plants, but I can't believe that. I can not believe people could be that selfish.

Things are soooo complicated. I wish I could go back to a simpler time when all I worried about was making documentaries.

Love,
Louise

12
TALLULAH

Tallulah Hand was having a crisis. Her boyfriend had just left her for a younger woman who ran triathlons. Her Vanderbilt Lady Commodores tennis team had just lost an embarrassing series to the University of Tennessee, with a series against Texas coming up, which would be doubly embarrassing to Tallulah, since that is where she had been an All-American in her college years.

Plus, she had gained ten pounds, and for the first time in her five-foot-eleven-inch life she was trying to stay on a diet.

Plus, she hated living in Nashville, which had become a huge, sprawling mess of a city, where rivers of automobiles crawled at all times of day except for a few hours right before dawn.

Tallulah got up from her desk at the Currey Tennis Center, having decided to walk to a sports store three miles away to buy a ten-speed bicycle.

"Fuck Carter Angell and fuck his anorexic Italian girlfriend. Let them triathlon themselves into the sunset," she said. "I'm making some moves and I'm making them fast."

Tallulah stuck her cell phone into the side pocket of her dark green carpenter pants, added a Visa card, a driver's license, and some cash, and walked out of the building without locking the door to her office.

She had made it to the edge of the campus when the cell phone rang. She pulled it out and answered it.

"Hello, hello," Olivia said. "What's going on? I'm in bed trying to keep my baby inside my womb. I'm bored to death. Tell me news. I saw the scores of the Tennessee matches. Was it as bad as it sounds on paper?"

"They don't play," Tallulah said. "There's not a single woman on the team who really goes after it. I can't inspire them. All they want is the scholarships and the uniforms."

"Well, that's a waste of your talent. Where are you?"

"I'm on the front of the campus near the old administration building, manicured lawns, flower beds, and trees so old they were big when the Fugitive poets walked here. I love this part of the campus. I think

249

about John Crowe Ransom when I'm under these trees. All those guys were committing adultery with one another's wives. Most of the great poems came from that. Carter dumped me, by the way. He moved in with a triathlete from Colorado. They were training together."

"What's the good news?"

"That he wasn't living in my house. That I hated his fucking dog, and that I'd be relieved if I hadn't been dumped."

"What's the weather like today in Nashville, Tennessee?"

"Gorgeous, spring, new leaves on old trees, flowers, daisies, tulips. It's the end of exam week. The campus is getting emptied. My girls are mad because they have to go to Austin Monday. They should be. They're going to be annihilated. My old coaches there will get to watch me watch that."

"So are you going to stay depressed or not?"

"I'm walking to a sports store to buy an all-terrain bicycle and then I'm going to ride it home and eat my diet lunch. I got fat, Olivia. I had no idea how unpleasant it is to have your clothes be too tight. I'm doing Sugar Busters. I started yesterday."

"Why don't you go down to a black high school and volunteer to teach a couple of days a week during their summer school? You might find a Venus Williams."

"That's an idea. How'd you come up with that?"

"I have to stay in bed; staying still is cranking up parts of my brain that I haven't used in a while. I've been mindfucking about our young people never lending a hand in the world. Service, the thing our old Presbyterian ministers used to preach every Sunday. It's something the Cherokees assume all people know, and the ones who don't drink always practice it, and not just the women — the men do too."

"Einstein said he tried to constantly remember that his life was based on the work and hands of thousands of men and women over hundreds of years, and that he must strive to pay that back in whatever measure he could."

"Hiroshima? Nagasaki? Well, that wasn't his fault. He was afraid Hitler would get there first."

"Now North Korea, India, Pakistan, Israel, France, Germany, England, the United States, China — who else? I used to try to keep track of nuclear problems."

"Don't you get to take free classes at Vanderbilt?"

"Yes."

"Have you taken any?"

"No."

"Well, there you are. Get out of the box. You don't have to be a losing tennis coach twenty-four-seven, do you?"

"I'm on West End Avenue, passing hundreds of automobiles going ten miles an hour, ruining the air, burning up the fossil fuels your husband is fighting to secure. I have to go ten more blocks past this sixth level of Hades and then I can cut through some rich neighborhoods where there's more oxygen. I'm glad you called. You couldn't have called me at a single moment when I wanted to talk to you more than I do today."

"Come visit. Come sit by my bedside."

"I might. Don't be surprised if I do. I might just leave from Austin if they lose as badly as I think they are going to. I won't fly home with them. That's a message."

"Come on, then. I'm not going anywhere for at least another week."

"I might. Actually, I probably will. Don't be surprised if I show up."

Sunday morning headlines. Twenty-eight Iraqis killed, forty-eight wounded, in insurgent attacks in Baghdad and Tikrit. The tally for the week, eight American dead, including three contractors.

Two hundred and sixteen bodies found in a mass grave, making the genocide count in Iraq somewhere in the range of sixty thousand. How are there any people left there? Olivia wondered.

"I'm turning off all news media for twenty-four hours," Olivia told Mary Lily when she brought in her breakfast tray. "And I'm getting out of this bedroom and staying out of it. I called the Merry Maids. They'll be here at ten o'clock to clean the house. My cousin might be coming from Nashville."

"I could clean the house. I know how."

"Yeah, but you don't like to do it."

"I might go home for a few days, since your cousin's coming," Mary Lily said. "If you can do without me."

"Go on. I know you're tired of being here."

"Well, if you'll be all right. Philip would come to get me. He said just to call."

"Call him. The Merry Maids will be here at noon. I'll have people here all day." Olivia sat up in the bed, put her feet on the floor, and walked across the room and back three times before she sat down to eat the delicious breakfast Mary Lily had prepared for her. It was a small waffle with scrambled eggs and bacon. There was a pot of herb tea with cream and sugar. There was a yellow tulip in a white vase. "Riches," Olivia said, looking toward her aunt. "I live like a princess."

Bobby Tree had been at work since six that morning, which was still night in Tikrit, Iraq. The unmanned helicopter he was piloting from a console at Nellis Air Force Base was hovering over an office building in Tikrit, watching the back entrances while a team of Marine Special Operations soldiers were coming in the front. They were searching for the insurgents who had carried out four car bombings the day before. A tip from a sixteen-year-old Iraqi boy had led them to the office building. A marine in an armored vehicle in front of the building was directing Bobby as he worked the helicopter nearer to the building, spotted the men escaping through the rear doors carrying weapons, shot three of them, and wounded two more.

Then it was over. The marines had taken the building, and dogs were searching for explosives or bombs. Ten more insurgents were in custody. The bodies of the dead were in the courtyard where the helicopter's guns had left them.

Bobby sat back in his chair, spread his hands out to stretch his fingers, and then put his hands back on the controls and moved the helicopter higher and to the side of the building, where it would be out of the range of handheld missile launchers.

May 23, 2005. Tallulah Hand boarded the Northwest Airlines regional jet to Austin, Texas, and settled into her seat to finish reading *Tennis* magazine. "I should go to the Italian Open," she said under her breath. "I played it twice and lost in the first round both times. But I was there."

Philip Whitehorse parked his truck in the driveway, threw the stuff that was piled in the front passenger seat into the back of the vehicle, brushed the seat off with his black denim jacket, and then heaved a sigh and took the cigarettes out of his shirt pocket and stuck them in the glove compartment.

He combed his short hair with an old comb he kept on the floor of the front seat, then got out and went up Olivia's front steps to collect Mary Lily and take her back to Tahlequah. He'd missed her, and that worried him more than he wanted to admit. When she was in Tahlequah he only saw her a couple of nights a week, but since she had been in Tulsa taking care of Olivia, he had been thinking about her every night. He'd even thought about her while he was watching the Kentucky Derby. That was the last straw.

"Here comes Philip Whitehorse," Olivia yelled down to her aunt. "He's coming up the front walk." Olivia was sitting on the edge of the bed, looking out the window. She was only staying in bed half the day now. Her doctor said she could get up for good the following week. She was pushing that by sitting on the side of the bed half the time when she was in it. She had had it with staying in bed and acting like an invalid, although it had the effect of making her sympathetic to injured and bedridden people, and she was planning on writing a column about the courage of ordinary people in the face of serious illnesses and injuries.

Mary Lily walked down the stairs and opened the front door and stood waiting while Philip removed his hat and came through the door. "I'm mighty glad you're coming home," Philip said. "I had to watch the derby alone. Kayo was watching it with your granddad and Spotted Horse Woman."

"They didn't ask you to watch it with them?"

"Not that I noticed," he said.

"Well, I'm about ready. Come in and sit down and I'll get my suitcase." She had decided to stop looking at him. Enough was enough in the sentimental department, especially at their age. "You want to go upstairs and talk to my niece?"

"I think we need to get going. It's going to rain soon. I'd like to get back before it starts."

"All right, then." Mary Lily walked back upstairs, told Olivia good-bye, collected her small suitcase, and walked back down the stairs. Philip took the suitcase from her and they walked together down the path to the driveway and got into the truck without talking anymore.

Olivia watched them from the side of the window so they couldn't see her. She was laughing so hard she couldn't stop. She was laughing harder than she had laughed in months. It was May 24, 2005, and for once she was thinking about something besides people being shot and killed in Iraq and Afghanistan, and children living without their parents because of AIDS or the tsunami.

As soon as she could quit laughing, she

walked out of the bedroom, went into her office, opened her computer, and began to write a column for Tuesday's newspaper.

"It is late spring," the column began. "Time to count our blessings and read poetry, time to go to graduations and think about the future. Time for mind opening and reevaluation.

"Here is a poem I have been meaning to print in the paper for several years. It is by the great American poet Robert Frost.

Spring Pools

These pools that, though in forests, still
    reflect
The total sky almost without defect,
And like the flowers beside them, chill and
    shiver,
Will like the flowers beside them soon be
    gone,
And yet not out by any brook or river,
But up by roots to bring dark foliage on.

The trees that have it in their pent-up buds
To darken nature and be summer
    woods —
Let them think twice before they use their
    powers
To blot out and drink up and sweep away

These flowery waters and these watery
  flowers
From snow that melted only yesterday.

"A poet is a painter," Olivia wrote, "giving us images so beautifully worded that they have the power to become engraved upon our hearts.

"When I was in school, my English teachers gave us poetry to read and memorize. Teachers don't have time for that sort of thing anymore. So if you want your children to have this sort of richness in their lives, it's going to be up to you to teach it to them."

13
OPERATION MATADOR

Bobby Tree got off work at 10 p.m., Mountain time. He had been at the console cluster since five that morning. Missiles he had fired and bombs he had dropped had killed seventeen insurgents and destroyed four buildings.

He closed up his books for the day, refused a friend's offer to go out for a beer, drove to his quarters, took off most of his clothes, sat on the floor in what he hoped was a position of prayer, and tried to align himself with the forces of good in the world. He prayed, in some imitation of prayer he had learned from twenty years' devotion to *Star Wars* movies.

He was hungry but didn't feel like eating. He was elated and hated the elation. He was tired but didn't want to sleep.

It was too late to call Olivia. He was afraid he might wake her.

At eleven thirty his cell phone rang. He found it in his pants pocket and answered it.

"Are you all right?" Olivia asked. "I was watching the news. Were you part of this?"

"Yes."

"Congratulations, then."

"For what?" he answered. "I'm tired, honey. It's weird; this whole deal is weird. I'm glad you called."

"I'm coming in a few weeks," she said. "To stay for a while. We need to find an apartment. I'm not staying here when you're there doing what you are doing."

"I'm glad," he answered. "I need you here."

Bobby woke at five the next morning, got up, made coffee, and lay his uniform out on the unmade bed. He didn't have to clock in until six and it was only a ten-minute drive from his off-base two-bedroom apartment to his post.

He poured a cup of coffee and walked out the front door to look at the skies. There were dark clouds above the mountains, with lightning running through them like the paintings the Pueblo Indians made on their arms and foreheads. It never meant rain.

Bobby had learned that weeks before. You could expect rain for days in the desert and it would never fall. Prick teasers, the natives called the lightning-filled clouds in the distance. Bobby often wished Little Sun Wagoner would come out here to visit. He'd find something to say about this landscape. He'd know why men would choose to live here instead of moving where there was water.

Bobby went back into his house, opened a cabinet, took out a breakfast bar and opened it, and began to eat. He opened the refrigerator and took out milk and orange juice and poured both into glasses and drank part of each, then put half of the breakfast bar on the table and hurried into his bedroom and dressed. He put on his boots and tied the laces, brushed his teeth and combed his short hair, and then left the house in a hurry.

His ten-year-old Land Rover was parked by the side of the apartment, and he got into it and drove off with all the windows rolled down and a Waylon Jennings CD belting out cowboy songs.

The old Land Rover was undependable in the radiator department, but Bobby rode the machine the way he would a skittish mare. He watched the gauges and he carried a plastic can of antifreeze in the front seat. So far, he had made it to work every day. It was five 5:45 when he arrived at the gate of the base and stuck his card into the slot before driving through. At 5:55 he was sliding into his console beside an officer who had been there all night.

"What's happening?" he asked.

"We flattened a house full of people," the man said. "At least two hundred insurgents got away and we're looking for them. I'm glad you're here. I'm leaving as soon as your copilot comes. I left all the data in the file." The man stood up, stretched his legs, and went to stand at the door to the console cluster. Bobby's copilot came in and took his place. They went to work guiding a very small drone over a six-mile square of desert in the dark.

In Baghdad a man whose family was being held hostage in a small village walked into a checkpoint and blew himself up, killing two American soldiers and wounding thirty-four Iraqi policemen.

In Tikrit the third cousin of one of the men Bobby had shot from the unmanned helicopter set to work threading a long, thin hose filled with plastic explosives into a tunnel leading to a group of abandoned houses

Names of the Dead

The Department of Defense has identified 1,610 American service members who have died since the start of the Iraq war. It confirmed the deaths of the following Americans yesterday:

CASTLE, Samuel T., 26, Staff Sgt., Army; Naples, Tex.; 327th Signal Battalion, Thirty-fifth Signal Brigade.

DAVIDS, Wesley G., 20, Lance Cpl., Marine Reserves; Dublin, Ohio; Fourth Marine Division.

GIVENS, Steven R., 26, Specialist, Army; Mobile, Ala.; Third Infantry Division.

IVY, Kendall H. II, 28, Staff Sgt., Marines; Crawford, Ohio; Second Marine Division.

SCHMIDT, John T. III, 21, Lance Cpl., Marines; Brookfield, Conn.; Second Marine Division.

SMITH, John M., 22, Sgt., Army; Wilmington, N.C.; Second Squadron, Eleventh Armored Cavalry.

near the highway that runs from the police headquarters into the town. He had been at his job for three days. It would take him three more. Then he would be transported to the Baghdad area, where he would begin work on the airport highway there. He was thirty-six years old and had been born in Saudi Arabia but had lived in Syria most of his life. Twenty-six of his male relatives had died fighting for various groups who opposed the governments of three countries. It was a way of life for his family. It was their business. At thirty-six he was one of the oldest living men in his family, but he never thought about such things. He would have had a hard time saying with assurance the year in which he was born, and he had long since forgotten the day. What he loved to do, and was good at, was figuring out ways to introduce plastic explosives into places where they could be set off so as to kill the largest number of people at the most unexpected moments. Every time the enemy figured out one of his devices, he went to work to invent another one. He had no money and no women, and he wanted none. He had his work and he loved to do it and he did it. He had not heard about his cousin's death in Tikrit and would not have mourned if he had known.

■ ■ ■ ■

In Austin, Texas, the Lady Commodores tennis team from Vanderbilt University had the Lady Longhorns from the University of Texas tied 6–6 in singles and were battling it out in doubles. A young woman from Memphis whom Tallulah Hand had recruited the year before was leading the charge. She had won two of the singles matches and was about to win her second doubles match. She was on fire. She had come into her own. A dressing-down Tallulah had given her on the airplane ride to Austin had sunk in, grown tentacles, and taken over her psyche. She was playing the doubles match with blisters on her feet and a shoulder problem that would keep her from serving a tennis ball for six months after the match, but she was playing through the pain. She was in love with Tallulah for inspiring her to these heights. It was the first time since she had been at Vanderbilt that she was happy. In fact, she was more than happy. She was ecstatic. Every now and then she would glance up into the Lady Commodores box and see Tallulah watching her, and she would tighten her grip on her racket and serve another perfectly placed ace or race to the net to smash a return at the feet of her opponent.

When the score was 5–1 in the second set, Tallulah took out her cell phone and called Olivia. "My girls are playing tennis," she said. "We're about to beat Texas for the first time in three years. This will get me a raise, if not the crown I deserve. So I can't come to see you. You doing all right?"

"Hooray," Olivia answered. "Yeah, I'm fine. I called some people to clean the house because I thought you were coming, and I got rid of my aunt for a few days, so you helped me whether you show up or not. Of course, Dad's still here, but he's staying at a hotel."

"I got to hang up. Sorry. Love you. See you soon, I hope."

Tallulah hung up the telephone and started concentrating on watching the faces of her old coaches as they watched her team defeat their team. Today I like my job, Tallulah decided. Tomorrow I might hate it. Who gives a damn in a finite world. Next semester I'll take geology or astrophysics. It's nice at Vanderbilt. I think I'll stay.

14
SLEEPING SWORDS

More than 620 people, including 58
U.S. troops, have been killed since April
28, when insurgents launched a bloody
campaign. . . .
During the same period, there have
been at least 89 car bombs killing at least
355 people, according to the AP count.
— Paul Garwood, Associated Press,
May 25, 2005

At the end of May, four thousand Iraqi
troops mounted an offensive against the
foreign fighters who had been blowing up
people and infrastructure for the past ten
months with little to stop them.
In the battles, five different kinds of
unmanned aircraft assisted in the destruc-
tion of insurgent strongholds.
"We have to train their soldiers to call in
the drones," Bobby's superior officer told
him. "I'm sending four people from here to

help train them. You're one of them. You'll be second in command of the group."

"When do we leave, sir?" Bobby answered.

"Next week. Maybe Wednesday, if we can get transport. We'll have meetings and briefings every day until then. I'm going with you for a few days; then I'll come back. You may be over for a year."

"You sound funny," Olivia said when she talked to him that night on the telephone. "What's going on?"

"Something I can't talk about."

"You're going there," she said.

"I wish you could come out here, baby," he answered. "But you can't. So is your dad still there?"

"Yeah. But he's staying at a hotel. It makes him nervous to stay around here long. He doesn't have anything to do."

"Don't start worrying," Bobby said. "I'll call you as soon as I know what I can say."

"I'll figure it out by then. I bet you a hundred dollars I can figure it out before you call."

"I wouldn't want to bet money against you. How about letting me name the baby if I win?"

"I wouldn't win anything betting that. The mother always gets to say what the baby is named."

"I want him to have a Cherokee name and a regular name like Max or Sam or Will or maybe Daniel after your dad."

"Okay, then bet me."

"Okay, I will."

Olivia was in her bed. As soon as she hung up the phone, she started yelling to Mary Lily, who had just returned to Tulsa. "Bobby's going over there," she said. "I know it. You should have heard his voice. He was excited about it. I swear he was."

"What did he say?" Mary Lily asked.

"Nothing. He doesn't know yet what he can tell me. Get me a computer. I'll figure it out. Get me the one on the chair."

Mary Lily handed Olivia the thin, flat silver computer, and Olivia started researching all the data the Pentagon had released in the past few days. Half an hour later she had found nothing she didn't already know. Troop deployments were announced every Friday.

"Come eat breakfast with me," she told her father when she got him on the phone at his hotel. "I need you. I think Bobby is being sent over there. I can't figure out what for, though, and I'm getting worried. It isn't good for this baby if I worry."

"What time do you get up?"

"Come at seven. I'll be up by then."

"I'll be there."

"Bring in the papers and buy me *USA Today* on your way over. I think they give it away at hotels."

"I'll be there."

Daniel hung up the telephone and fell down on his knees beside the bed to pray. He was a devout Episcopalian who believed in God in a very old-fashioned way. The older his children became, the more he found himself praying to his God. Things he would never have dreamed of asking for for himself he prayed for fervently for his children. Hostages to fortune, he told himself this night. That's what my sister Anna said they were. Some guy called Bacon wrote it down and she read it. She said that was why she was glad she never had any children, except she wasn't glad and if she had had them she wouldn't have killed herself just because she got cancer.

Bobby called Olivia back at nine the next morning just as Olivia and Mary Lily and Daniel were finishing the waffles Mary Lily had made for breakfast.

"I'm going to Baghdad to train Iraqi foot

soldiers to call in the drones when they need them," he said. "My colonel's going for a couple of weeks, as well as more men from here. And an Iraqi psychologist from the University of Michigan, who's going to figure out which ones of them are spies. I'm not going to be in danger, Olivia. I probably won't ever leave the compound."

"All right."

"How are you doing? When do you see the doctor again?"

"In three days. She might let me get up. I'm afraid to weigh myself. I bet I've gained ten pounds."

"I'm not going to be in danger, Olivia. So I guess I won the bet, then."

"I guess you did." Olivia turned to her father and her aunt. "He gets to name the baby. I lost a bet."

"Tell your granddaddy to start looking for a Cherokee name," Bobby said. "One that everyone else hasn't already named someone. Look, I have to go. I'll talk to you tonight."

"Can I do anything?" Daniel asked when Olivia had hung up the telephone.

"Yes," she said. "I have a detailed map of the Middle East; I want you to take it to Kinko's and get it blown up into a wall-size poster, the bigger the better. And I want a blown-up map of Baghdad also. I'll have to find one. You might have to go by the paper and pick one up."

"Whatever you want," Daniel said. "Whatever I can do."

Bobby called Olivia three more times before he left. All three calls were short. In none of them did either Olivia or Bobby say what they were feeling; nor did Bobby tell her more about what he was going to be doing in Iraq or where or when.

Later she would be glad she had not known, as she might have repeated it to someone in some way.

"So did your granddad ever come up with a name?" Bobby asked in the last conversation they had.

"He said he had an ancestor named Vitochuco who almost killed de Soto by summoning the power of a great bird and turning his arms into wings. He said they used to call men in his family Vito when they wanted to praise them for their courage. I thought that sounded pretty good. Vito Tree. What do you think?"

"I like that. Yeah, I like that a lot. It would be a good name if he wanted to rodeo."

"Well, he sure as hell isn't going to rodeo. If you think I'm ruining my body to bring a son into the world so he can break all his bones in the rodeo, you're wrong."

"Yeah, after we get him, I guess we'll just keep him in the house and watch him."

"We better put Vitochuco on the birth certificate or people will think he's Italian."

"Daniel Vitochuco Tree. I guess that's about it, then. I'd like to stop worrying about it, so that's okay with me if it's okay with you."

"When are you leaving Nevada?"

"In the next day or so. They don't announce it ahead of time. They're all careful as hell about that kind of information, especially when there's a senior officer on the trip."

"Okay, then."

"I love you, baby."

"And me you. Take care of yourself."

"I will."

Forty-seven hours and six minutes later, the armored vehicle Bobby was riding in on the road into Baghdad from the airport came under fire from insurgents, swerved to avoid a car driven into the road, and was blown up by a hand-thrown grenade made in Ohio and stolen by insurgents from an ammunition dump in Pakistan three years before. The colonel escaped with superficial wounds, as did both soldiers riding in the backseat. The driver and Bobby were killed so quickly they didn't have time to finish going into shock or scream or be in pain or care.

Little Sun had been restless all night. Finally he had gotten out of bed at four in the morning and gone out to the earth island to sit cross-legged on the mound and watch the waxing moon slip behind the line of trees to the east of the mound. There were many stars still in the sky and they all foretold disaster. Not all the beauty of the earth in early June, not the new full growths of leaves or the wildflowers blooming or the cherry trees laden with fruit or the smell of honeysuckle or the knowledge that deer were in the woods waiting to walk out to the pond and drink the cold clear water from the springs, not the song of early morning birds could erase what Little Sun knew.

When it was light he got up, shook out his old legs, and walked back to the house to wake Crow. "We must go to Olivia," he told her. "Get up now. We must leave as soon as we can."

■ ■ ■ ■

The news came as it always comes. Two marine officers walked up the path to Olivia's house at seven fifteen in the morning and rang the doorbell, and Mary Lily and Philip Whitehorse, who had come over early to have breakfast before a rodeo showcase, went to the door. Daniel was reading the newspaper in the living room. Olivia was sitting on the edge of her bed, looking out the windows at the mockingbirds, and had seen the officers park the official-looking automobile and get out and begin to walk toward her house. She put on a pair of loose khaki pants and a shirt from the collection of maternity clothes her sister had sent her from New Orleans. She pulled her hair back in a ponytail and put on leather sandals and walked down the stairs to where her father and her aunt and the nephew of the man who had taught her to ride cutting horses stood with the two marine officers in the hall that led from the front door into the house.

All her life she would remember that moment, and the faces that were turned toward her, and how her first thought had been that she must not lose the child she was carrying

— her first thought because she had already gone into a denial so swift and terrible it would follow her to her grave. All her life she had denied that her mother was dead and that she had no mother. All her life she had denied that she had not known her father, and even after she found him, she denied that in the years before she knew him she had longed to know him. Now she denied that Bobby Tree was dead. She refused to acknowledge that Bobby was not going to come home or hold her in his arms or calm her down or call her on the telephone or be her husband or her friend or see his child or live with her.

"Come in," she said to the marine officers who were already in the hall. "You have brought us bad news, haven't you?"

"The president will want you to come to Washington to receive the medals," the officers said to her later.

"No," she answered. "I'm pregnant, and I've had trouble with the pregnancy. I cannot travel, not for many months. I'm the editor of the *Tulsa World,* our newspaper here. I'm on a leave of absence for the duration of the pregnancy. Please tell the president I am honored that he wants me to come there, but it is impossible at this time."

She was sitting on a black leather chair that was a copy of a Mies van der Rohe design, and she had not shed a tear or stopped for one moment thinking that she must keep her back straight and her shoulders square and her chin high.

The doorbell was ringing. "Excuse me," she said. "That might be my grandparents. My grandfather is an intuitive. He probably knew this before you did." She got up from the chair and went to the front door and opened it, and Crow held out her arms and Olivia hugged her fiercely, and then Little Sun came into the hall and took her hand and held it and they walked back into the living room to finish talking to the officers about when they would have a body to bury.

"Have you told Bobby's father?" Daniel asked the officers.

"They were looking for him," one of the officers answered. "I don't know if they have found him yet."

Many people left work to come to Olivia's house.

One of the first to arrive after Little Sun and Crow was Kathleen Whitman, Olivia's obstetrician. She took Olivia upstairs and examined her and told her she could stay up for four hours, as long as she went to bed for an hour in the afternoon and was careful about how many times she went up and down the stairs. "We'll start walking together next week," she said, looking deep into Olivia's eyes, for once being her physician more than her friend. "Can you get to the track by the hospital? It's a great new surface. I really need to start exercising again. I've gained eight pounds and my blood pressure's on the rise. It would be good for both of us. Can we plan on that?"

"Except for the funeral. I have to get through that, but it may be ten days before we have his body anyway. So yes, Wednesday morning at seven. I'll meet you there. Can you do that?"

"I'm going to do it. Physician, heal thyself, and so forth. You're the one who used to tell me that."

"Wednesday at seven, then. I'm going to get dressed. People will be coming over. Stay. I want you here."

Olivia got up from her bed and changed clothes, putting on a flowered sundress Jessie had sent her. It was white piqué with big red and yellow flowers and appliqué on the straps and a yellow grosgrain belt that tied in a bow at the side. She put on red sandals and went into the bathroom and brushed her hair and tied it back in a neater ponytail, and added the pearl earrings her father had given her the year she turned seventeen. Then she and Kathleen went downstairs to talk to people and thank them for coming to her house.

"How did they find out about it?" Olivia asked her father later, when the house was full of people.

"Mary Lily called your doctor," he said. "I don't know about the rest."

At ten o'clock, Daniel went into the television room and called Jessie and told her what had happened.

At eight that evening, Jessie arrived at the Tulsa Airport with her husband, King Mallison. They had left their children with her mother-in-law and come on the first plane they could get. It was surprisingly easy on Memorial Day to get an airplane from New Orleans to Tulsa, if you were able to fly first class, which they were now that King had joined his stepfather's law firm, which represented management in labor disputes.

They got to Olivia's house at nine fifteen that night. Jessie went upstairs and sat on the edge of Olivia's bed and held her hand until Olivia took the sleeping pill Kathleen had prescribed for her. After Olivia fell asleep, Jessie sat beside her sister in the darkened room. After a while, Mary Lily came into the room and sat on the other side of the bed. They stayed there for a long time, watching the sleeping widow. Before she left the room, Jessie picked up the flowered sundress and took it to the closet and hung it on a hanger, putting the little straps into the hanger clips so it would not fall on the floor.

15
BURYING THE DEAD

"The bodies are piling up," Louise said when Winifred called her with the news.

"Two dead, one wounded," Winifred answered. "That's not so many, and none of them were really kin to us. I mean, they aren't blood kin."

"Your husband's blood kin," Louise answered. "His blood is mingled with ours in my daughter. He's a perfect biological match to my husband, so he's kin to me."

"They're having a memorial at Nellis next week," Winifred said. "Bobby and the other man who died were from here, and a colonel and his aide are wounded. I don't know when it's going to be."

"What can we do to help Olivia?"

"Nothing. Any more than you could help me. It never goes away, not if you slept with them. I had slept with Charles. He was the first man who ever really loved me. He loved me when I was fat. He liked me fat as much as he liked me later."

"You weren't fat. Slightly overweight."

"Fifteen pounds overweight. It was all around my waist. I love Brian. I really deeply love him. But I love Charles too, and I will always love him and mourn for him." Winifred started crying, and Louise couldn't think of anything to say.

"Don't cry," she said at last. "Go for a walk. Cook something. Iron a blouse. E-mail Olivia."

"I've talked to her twice already. Okay, good-bye. I have to call some more people. I love you. I'll see you at the funeral, I guess, if not before."

They buried Bobby on a rise of land above the snakelike earth island Little Sun and Kayo had built to celebrate Bobby's wedding to Olivia. Little Sun and Crow had cleared the burial place years before. They had even planted a grove of cherry trees near the site and kept the pine trees from taking over by picking up the cones each spring. It was a small hill formed when melting glacier water came down over that part of Oklahoma and made the creek that flowed into the river and left the springs that made the pond beside the earth island. Deer lived among the trees behind the site, and at all seasons birds called in the trees and came down onto the cleared places to search for food left in the gullies after rains. Little Sun had thought he would be the first to be buried there, but now it would be the father of his great-grandchild instead.

"I want a headstone that can be seen from far away," Olivia said. "I like to see country graveyards with headstones sticking up. I want it to be some native stone from around these parts; maybe I'll find something later and we can have part of it polished so we can write his name and leave a place for mine. Anyway, if it's okay with you all, that's where I want to bury him." She was talking to his father, Bud Tree, who had come to her house two days after Bobby died and cried a lot while she talked to him. "He loved you a lot, Bud," she went on. "He was proud of you. I was thinking I might put one of his buckles in the casket. I guess we'll bury him in his marine uniform. What do you think? I don't know when they'll send him to us or what he will be wearing."

"You do whatever you want to do," Bud said. "I'd be proud to have him buried on your granddad's place. Anything's okay with me."

They buried Bobby at ten o'clock in the

morning on a hot early June day. The hill beside Little Sun's pasture was filled with all the people who had come to the wedding, plus many more, including Olivia's cousins from North Carolina and their husbands, and her sister Jessie and Jessie's husband, and her uncle Niall and her aunt Helen and her aunt Louise and both their husbands. Her cousin Winifred's husband, Brian, and her cousin Louise's husband, Carl, both stood with the color guard, and a marine played bagpipes, and then four dancers from the Cherokee Nation danced the death rites and laid their spears beside the coffin, and a Baptist minister and a Cherokee medicine man said prayers, and then the coffin was lowered into the grave, and Bud Tree walked up to the grave, and took up the first shovel, and then the men of the tribe began to cover the coffin with the hard red clay of eastern Oklahoma, of the Cherokee Nation.

Some of the Hand family stayed in Tahlequah for several days. Olivia's uncle Niall came out to the Wagoner farm very early the next morning to sit with Little Sun and Bud Tree beside the grave, and to watch while Roper Wagoner and his sons hauled the huge piece of limestone that Olivia had found in a back pasture to the gravesite and set it into the ground above the grave. A man from Muskogee was coming to smooth a place on the stone to write the names of people buried below it.

The grave was still covered by the flowers the funeral home had brought in the hearse with the coffin that held Bobby's patched-together body dressed in his marine dress uniform. The belt buckles from his first two rodeos were beside his right hand, as though he might need to rise up and use them for weapons if evil spirits came to disturb his rest.

Bud Tree and Niall Hand and Little Sun took the flowers and carried them deep into the woods and spread them beneath the trees. They took the small painted sticks that had held the flowers together, and the ribbons that were attached to the flowers, and the envelopes with messages from people who loved Olivia and Bobby printed by the hands of people in florist shops in Tulsa and Tahlequah. Niall kept the cards that had been in the envelopes to give to Olivia, and they took the rest of the debris and made it into a small pile near the earth island, and Little Sun knelt beside it and added cedar bark he crushed into powder with his hands and set it on fire. The small plume of smoke rose straight up into the hot, windless morning, and the men left it burning and went back to the gravesite to help Roper and his sons unload the huge, jagged, rectangular piece of limestone Olivia had found.

"I would have put him in a tree the way the old Indians used to do," she told her cousin Louise, "but it's against the law. Anyway, now I have to get back to work and I have to make sure this baby comes into the world proud and strong and ready to have his life. At least I don't have to name him some corny fucking name now. Bobby wanted to name him all sorts of crazy things, but I'm going to name him Robert Daniel Tree. So what are you doing in Washington? Are you getting anything done for your work?"

"I'm taking care of Carla Louise. You can't get anything done when you have kids. It's the wildest thing, how much energy she sucks out of me."

"I'm glad you brought her. I liked having children at the funeral. It made it seem as if we have a real family and not just a bunch of people spread out all over the United States talking to each other on cell phones and e-mailing each other."

"We have a family," Louise said. "Uncle Niall's going to have us a family reunion.

He's been working on it for months."

"When are you all going back?"

"Carl and I are leaving from Tulsa tomorrow morning at eleven."

"I might ride back with you." Olivia stood up and stretched her arms over her head. "I've got to get home and get to work on my life. I can't hang around Tahlequah acting like a widow. Where are the men? Where's Carl?"

"They're out in your granddad's pasture, moving that stone you found and doing things to the grave. They're all, well, more morbid, I guess you could say. Uncle Niall went out yesterday morning to help move the flowers into the woods. If I was still into photographing graveyards, I would have had a camera going on this production. Sorry, I don't mean to sound, well, disrespectful."

"Bobby would be laughing his head off if he could see all this. All his workers and his partner crying and all of that."

"If you want to go with us tomorrow, we'll be glad to come out to the farm and pick you up."

"I'll be ready at eight. Any time you get here is all right with me."

At nine thirty the next morning, Olivia was back at her house in Tulsa, alone, as she had insisted she wanted to be. As soon as Louise and Carl left, she went to the phone and called Kathleen and told her to meet her in the morning at the track. Then she called her cleaning lady and told her to come over and help her pack Bobby's clothes to send to the Goodwill.

Then she went into the bedroom that had been her office before Mary Lily moved in, and started turning it back into an office.

At noon she called Big Jim Walters and told him she wanted to come to the newspaper and work three days a week, and he said, "Hooray. When do you start?"

"Tomorrow," she said. "I'm in good health; nothing's wrong with me. I'll be in by eight."

16
AUGUST

Sunday afternoon. Olivia and Little Sun and Crow and Mary Lily were in Olivia's living room. Crow and Mary Lily were sitting on the red leather chaise, Little Sun was sitting on the blue chair, and Olivia was cuddled up in the double papasan chair she and Bobby Tree had bought one afternoon right after he moved into her house and before they decided to get married. The eight-month-old baby boy in Olivia's womb was lying on his side, listening and sucking on his left thumb. He had sucked it so much that when he was born he was going to be a quick learner in the sucking milk department, so quick he would astonish the nurses, not the last time he would acquire a trick with which to astonish women. For now, however, he was content to suck his thumb and listen to the voices and the sounds matter makes in space.

"I dreamed last night that Mother returned to me," Olivia said. "It was morning in the dream and I looked out the kitchen window and a parade was coming down the hill, friends of mine and kinsmen, and Bobby was there. Mother was in a wheelchair, but she was pretty and happy to see me. She was smiling and not young like in the photographs, but older, with a round face and hair pulled back like mine. She was very happy, as if she knew she was giving me a great gift to return to me in such good health and the right age to be my mother now that I am older."

"Bobby was with her too?" Crow asked. Ever since Bobby died, Crow and Little Sun and Mary Lily had been driving to Tulsa on Sunday afternoons to visit for a few hours; then they'd drive back. If Olivia was busy at the newspaper, they went to museums or had ice cream cones at the mall and watched the skaters on the indoor ice-skating rink and then drove home. Little Sun had bought a new car for these trips, a Toyota Camry with a sun roof and a CD player.

"Bobby was pushing her wheelchair, but Momma was not a cripple. He was just pushing her to be nice."

"Did they speak to you?" Little Sun asked.

"No. They just went on down the hill, in a good mood and happy, and then I woke up and it was dawn, and I thought about the dream all day and wrote it down when I went in to the office."

"Next time they will speak to you," Crow said.

"They came to tell you they are all right," Little Sun answered.

"They came to see if you were all right," Mary Lily put in.

"I have had such dreams," Crow added, "but never one in which two dead people are together, smiling at me."

"It wasn't the first dream," Olivia said. "Well, I'm starving. Let's put that food on the table." She got up and Mary Lily joined her and they went into the kitchen and began to fix supper. Crow had brought bowls of tomatoes and corn and green beans and a baked chicken, and they warmed those in the microwave and made biscuits. It was the first time her family had agreed to stay and eat supper when they came for a Sunday visit.

"You need to spend the night and drive home in the morning," Olivia said. "I don't want you driving home in the dark."

"There is a full moon and many stars. It is nice to drive home in darkness in the Toyota," Little Sun said.

Olivia sat down in her chair. The baby was beginning to move around, as he often did when there were people talking. "The baby's listening to us," she said. "He gets excited when people are talking. I wish you could have seen Momma's face in my dream. It was shining with happiness. It made me happy."

"That is why they came." Little Sun turned to Crow. "We will stay here tonight. She wants us to stay."

"Yes," Crow said.

After they ate dinner, they went out to the backyard and sat on the dilapidated yard furniture a former owner had left there, and Olivia finished telling them about her dreams of the past two months. "At first it was Bobby, all blown up but still in one piece, and he wanted me to help him find a place to be buried, and I tried to help him. Then he came and he was the way he used to be and I wanted to lie down with him, but it was not possible, and he said not to be sad, but I was sad and I cried in the dream, and when I woke I cried some more. Then one night he came and took my hand, and I knew that was all there was and all there would ever be. I think he said, 'Take care of our baby.' I told him that when I

293

heard he was dead, that was the first thing I thought, and he said that was good and not to feel bad about it."

Little Sun and Crow looked at each other and then they both got up and went to Olivia and stood beside her. "Let's go back in the house now," Little Sun said. "I will think about these dreams and tell you what I think. Many times the dead come to help us understand their leaving. It is good you are having dreams. I am glad to hear about this."

They went back into the house, and Olivia moved her papers from the bed in her office and turned down the covers for her grandparents and then went into the second bedroom to help Mary Lily put sheets on the smaller bed.

"It is the first time your grandfather has slept away from home in many years," Mary Lily said.

"I know." Olivia giggled, and Mary Lily started giggling with her. "That's why he has lived so long in good health. I hope he will be comfortable in there."

"If the bed is hard, he will like it," Mary Lily said. "If not, he will get up and sleep on the floor." They started giggling again and finished making up Mary Lily's bed, and then Olivia went into her own room and put on her nightgown and got into her bed and fell asleep almost before she could turn off the light.

"I had not known how hard it is to sleep in this house all alone," she told them in the morning, "until I slept all those hours without moving because you were here with me."

"So what do you think that all means?" Kathleen Whitman asked. It was two mornings later. Olivia had met Kathleen at the track beside the hospital at six in the morning, and they were finishing their fourteenth lap on the quarter-mile track.

"That I'm going to start believing in ghosts, obviously. Only they are not like ghosts. They are very lifelike and they don't stay long. I know they are figments of my imagination. I know that. I keep thinking Aunt Anna will appear next, wearing her wet garments, although they'll be perfectly preserved, I guess, the way they are in *The Tempest*. It is comforting to me, Kathleen. Really comforting. I guess I think it means they aren't really dead."

"We don't know anything except the small fraction of reality our five senses allow us to know. Well, we have stretched that out to the Hubble Space Telescope, and our microscopes get better and better and we can see inside cells and inside your womb. If I wanted to, I could do an amnio and tell you so much about that baby boy it would scare us both. I could take your DNA and his DNA and tell you if he'd have a bad temper."

"Except I already know who he is, better than your instruments could ever tell me. I know this baby like I know myself, Kathleen. I always have, ever since the day Bobby went to the drugstore and got the kit and told me I had to pee. He said, 'You have to urinate — I mean, pee.' I thought that was hilarious."

"You never cry over him?" They had slowed down their pace. Now they almost stopped, and Olivia looked at her friend.

"I cried in my sleep one night because I wanted to fuck him, and he told me we couldn't do it anymore."

"I wish you'd see a psychiatrist for a while. Your insurance would pay for six or seven visits. I might get them to stretch it out for more. Would you do it if I arrange it? It can't hurt, and it might help."

"I don't know, Kathleen. I'm a Cherokee Indian. We have people we can talk to."

"But not in Tulsa, Oklahoma, where you

live. Look, I have to stop now. I have to make rounds." They had come to the place where they left the track each morning. "I can't meet you tomorrow. I have surgery. But Friday I'll be here. Let me find you a psychiatrist. I don't want you talking to the dead and crying in your sleep. We've got a baby to get into the world. I want you wide awake, not off in some dreamworld."

"All right. I'll do it, then. Call me."

"I will. Good-bye."

Olivia got into her car and drove to the office and changed clothes in the ladies' room and then sat down at her computer and started trying to write a column that was due at four that afternoon.

"The names of the lost," it began. It ended, "How many deaths does it take till we know that too many people have died?"

"It's the best thing you've written all summer," Big Jim Walters said when he read it. "It's simple, clear. We'll get a lot of mail on this."

"You want to edit it?"

"No. It's just right. I'm jealous. I wish I'd written it."

17
BIRTH

Robert Daniel Sequoyah Tree was born at six in the afternoon on August 25. Olivia was at the hospital track with her obstetrician when her water broke, which they both thought was some hilarious, foreseen joke. Kathleen helped her across the street to the emergency entrance to the hospital and met her thirty minutes later in a labor room. Machines were hooked up to her womb and her arms. Machines monitored every process in her body. " 'All watched over / by machines of loving grace,' " Olivia told anyone who would listen. "Richard Brautigan, San Francisco, 1967. My mother was probably in the audience when he read the poem out loud. I have her autographed copy of the book at my house. Well, I'm getting giddy. What in the hell are you giving me?"

"Nothing," the young nurse answered. "Dr. Whitman hasn't given you anything yet. You're only dilated six centimeters. It will probably be hours before you deliver."

Daniel Hand got a telephone call an hour after Olivia was admitted to the hospital. He called his daughter Jessie and she called their cousins, and people started getting on airplanes and flying toward Tulsa. No one stopped and wondered if they ought to go there. They just got on planes and started going. "Uncle Niall won't have to have his reunion if stuff keeps happening with Olivia," Winifred told Louise. "I guess we'll just all keep meeting in Tulsa."

The baby arrived at six o'clock that afternoon. At eight, Daniel's plane arrived and was met by Philip Whitehorse. At ten the next morning, Louise and Jessie and Winifred arrived on flights from Washington, D.C., and New Orleans and Las Vegas. Tallulah Hand drove in from Nashville with a young landscape architect riding shotgun. He was six feet seven inches tall, had red hair, and was twenty-two years old. He was left-handed, had AB positive blood, and had quit Vanderbilt after two years to go into business for himself, doing yards in Nashville. His name was Manning Cash, and everyone kept saying to him, "One of our family names is Manning," and he kept answering, "Tallulah told me that."

Niall Hand arrived on an airplane at two the next afternoon and took a taxi to the hospital. He went to Olivia's room and kissed her on the forehead and gave her some roses he had bought in the Atlanta Airport. Then he gave her a box holding a small gold cross that had been her grandmother's.

"Go see the boy," Olivia said. "He's pretty cute. You'll like him."

Outside the nursery the rest of the visitors were clustered around a window, looking in at a small baby boy lying on his back with his arms extended. He was wearing a white cap with small royal blue bears on it. He was asleep.

"Look at the way he's sleeping," Tallulah said. "He's so laid back. Babies don't sleep like that. They sleep all cuddled up."

"Look at his black hair," Winifred said. "Isn't it pretty?"

"I can't see his hair," Niall said. "It's covered up with that cap."

"Can you believe everyone's here?" Louise asked. "Isn't this amazing?"

Later, when the family was settled in a hotel near the hospital, they met in Niall's room to make plans for dinner.

"Tallulah's grandmother's sister married a Manning," Niall explained to Manning Cash. "Even if he was a distant relative of yours, you wouldn't be related to her."

"I guess it got her interested in me, though," Manning answered. He was sticking close to Daniel and Niall. The rest of the family were too many women for him, as he had been raised in a family of six boys.

"I was interested in putting in some tulip beds," Tallulah said from across the room. "Besides, I always get interested in men who are redheaded and as tall as trees."

"Well, so what do you do in North Carolina?" Manning asked Niall. "What kind of work do you do?"

"Right now I'm running the governor's program for early childhood development," Niall said. "I got hooked into it because I went to school with the governor when we were young. It's the biggest bureaucratic mess you've ever seen in your life. You can't fire anyone, no matter how inept they are. It would put your life in jeopardy. I mean that. So I just keep plowing on and trying to make a difference, but it's a headache inside a circus inside a nightmare."

"He teaches kids to read and write and add and subtract and multiply and divide," Daniel said. "He's a saint. He thinks we can save the world. Do you think that, Manning?"

"I'm not sure if we can or not," Manning answered, "but I think we have to try."

"Susan's coming." Winifred came into the room. "Her plane gets in at eleven. I'm going to meet her. She's going to stay until Sunday. I got her a room next to mine. But I'll need a car."

"We'll go with you," Tallulah said. "I haven't seen Susan since she started being a surgeon. I want her to look at my knee."

At the hospital the nurse had just brought the baby in for Olivia to feed.

"I want to keep him in my room," Olivia said.

"Wait another day. The pediatrician wants you to stay here until Sunday night. We want to watch him another two days."

"Why?"

"She's always careful."

"He's eating," Olivia said. "Look at this. He's sucking it. Look at him suck."

The nurse leaned near to watch. She had orders from Dr. Whitman to stay in the room if Olivia was alone. "I don't want her getting emotional," Kathleen had said. "Her husband died in Iraq. I don't want her to have a chance to start getting sad."

The baby was sucking. He would suck on the teat until liquid filled his mouth, then let go of the teat while his mouth and tongue decided what to do with the liquid; then he rubbed his mouth around on Olivia's breast until he found the teat again, then sucked it some more. After three or four such adventures, he closed his eyes and fell into a small sleep while his digestive organs started working.

The nurse and Olivia watched each moment of this adventure with great attention.

"He's really good at it," the nurse said. "It usually takes them a few days to figure it out."

"Obsessive-compulsive, like everything we do," Olivia said. "Like learning to play tennis. It frustrates and maddens you, but as soon as you leave the court, your mind starts thinking about it and wants to try some more."

"Yeah, maybe. But this is about being hungry. That's more important than playing tennis."

"I get obsessed with things and forget to eat."

"Yeah, but you're not a baby."

The baby opened his eyes and stared at the two women a moment, then started moving his mouth around on the breast again, looking for the teat.

"So could someone get me a newspaper?" Olivia asked. "I haven't seen one in two days. I work for the *Tulsa World.* I really need to see a newspaper, if there's one around here."

At the hotel where Olivia's family were staying, the cousins had all gathered in the hotel dining room to have breakfast and make plans.

"We can't all leave at once," Tallulah said. "I can stay a few days, maybe until next weekend. I know a man at the university who will hit with me. And Manning wants to see some landscaping project he read about. So I'll be around a while. How about the rest of you?"

"I have to leave tonight," Jessie said. "I have to get home to my family. King wants me to come home."

"I'm going in the morning," Winifred said. "But I'll come back in a few weeks. I told her I was coming back."

"I'll stay with Tallulah," Louise said. "Carla Louise is happy as she can be with my mother-in-law. I'll stay until Olivia's home and we find an au pair or someone to help out."

"I'm going with Daniel to Tahlequah

tomorrow," Niall said. "I might be able to hang around a few days after that."

"I'm staying for a while," Daniel said. "I think she needs me here even if I'm not doing anything to help."

"Good for you, Daddy," Jessie said. "That's really good that you can see that." She went to him and put her hands on his shoulders and patted him as she would a child.

Turn the hearts of the parents to the children or the children to the parents, Niall was thinking. I think that's the New Testament, but it might be the old one. Anyway, it's sure a good idea. Which is why I won't say it doesn't take a genius to know to stay around when the daughter you didn't know you had until she was fifteen has a baby and her husband is only three months dead. Niall smiled and shook his head at the sight of his kinfolk gathered around a table trying to figure out how to help out in a tragedy, and doing a damn good crazy job of it too.

"I'll stay with you," he said to Daniel. "We might be of some use to someone. There's no reason to go running off before we get her settled."

"That little house she's in could use a better roof," Daniel answered. "And it's got to have a fence around the yard if she's going to stay there with the boy."

"The yard's a mess," Tallulah put in. "I noticed that when I came here for the wedding. Manning and I will look at it if you want us to. You can't just go putting up any kind of fence. There are fences now that add to a house's value, and they make these swing-set forts that match the fences."

"I'm going to the hospital," Louise said. "I want to see the baby again."

"I'll give her the swing set if you arrange to put it up," Jessie said. "King and Crystal and Manny want us to give her a really nice present for the baby. We love our swing set so much. They make such good ones now."

Crow and Little Sun and Mary Lily were at the hospital. They had left Tahlequah at seven and were in Olivia's room by nine. The lactation nurse left the room when they came in. Olivia was holding her sleeping son. "Do you want to hold him?" she asked her grandmother.

"No, I will watch you hold him."

"I want to hold him, but I'll wait until he's used to being here," Mary Lily said.

"We are proud of you, Granddaughter," Little Sun said. "You have made us very proud."

"Philip Whitehorse has gone to see the

lawyer who was the trickster at your blessing," Mary Lily said, lowering her chin so Olivia could not see her face. "He is going to have a divorce from his wife. This is the news I have for you."

"And then what will you do?" Olivia asked, smiling. "Will you go and live with him on Baron Fork and marry him?"

"I haven't thought what I will do," Mary Lily said. "Just because he is going to divorce his drunken wife doesn't mean I have to live on Baron Fork."

"Come hold this baby," Olivia said. "He knows your voice. He's been listening to me talk to you for months. Come on. He doesn't care if people hold him. All those nurses hold him and he isn't even kin to them." She held out the sleeping infant, and Mary Lily took him in her arms and sat beside Olivia's bed, looking down at his face and remembering his mother when they had placed Olivia in her care, so many years ago, but not that many really, just days and nights that had passed like a dream to lead them all to this day when there would be a new life to lead them on.

"What do you think?" Olivia asked.

"I think I'm glad to have him in the world with me."

"Would one of you go get me some newspapers?" Olivia asked. "No one in this place ever remembers to bring me the newspapers in the morning."

Little Sun got up and walked out of the room, went down on the elevator, bought three newspapers, and brought them back to Olivia's room.

It was August 27, 2005. The headlines read:

MAJOR HURRICANE FORMING IN GULF OF MEXICO

GOLD NEARS $500 AN OUNCE

ROBERTS HEARINGS TO BEGIN SEPT. 12

HAMAS WANTS CREDIT FOR GAZA PULLOUT

BESLAN RESIDENTS MOURN '04 ATTACK

INVESTIGATION CONTINUES INTO TUNISIAN PLANE CRASH OFF SICILY

EGYPT ARRESTS SUSPECTS IN RESORT BOMBINGS

U.S. CASUALTIES IN IRAQ REACH 1,866

December 20, 2006. As of this date, $300 *billion* has been spent by the United States on the war in Iraq. There have been 2,940 American casualties. Thousands have been seriously wounded, having lost eyes, ears, arms, legs, hands, feet, skin, blood, the ability to live life as healthy human beings. Pray that we care for them as we have promised that we would.

For some branches of the armed forces, the bonus for signing up for four years of service has reached as high as twenty and even thirty thousand dollars. The president announced on December 19, 2006, that he was raising a larger army.

A bumber sticker in Fayetteville, Arkansas, reads, "We are making enemies faster than we can kill them."

What in the hell are we supposed to do next?

— Excerpt from an editorial by
Olivia de Havilland Hand

ABOUT THE AUTHOR

Ellen Gilchrist, winner of the National Book Award for *Victory Over Japan,* is the author of more than twenty books, including novels, short stories, poetry, and a memoir. She lives in Arkansas.

The employees of Thorndike Press hope you have enjoyed this Large Print book. All our Thorndike and Wheeler Large Print titles are designed for easy reading, and all our books are made to last. Other Thorndike Press Large Print books are available at your library, through selected bookstores, or directly from us.

For information about titles, please call:
  (800) 223-1244

or visit our Web site at:
  http://gale.cengage.com/thorndike

To share your comments, please write:
  Publisher
  Thorndike Press
  295 Kennedy Memorial Drive
  Waterville, ME 04901